The Thrice Nar

Part XIV

Imperator

The Thrice Named Man

Part XIV

Imperator

by

Hector Miller

www.HectorMillerBooks.com

The Thrice Named Man

Part XIV

Imperator

All characters and events in this publication, other than those clearly in the public domain, are fictitious and any resemblance to real persons, living or dead, is purely coincidental.

Author: Hector Miller

Proofreading: Kira Miller

First edition, 2023, Hector Miller

Part XIV in the book series The Thrice Named Man

ISBN: 9798870666617

Text copyright © 2023 CJ Muller

All rights reserved.

No part of this publication may be reproduced, stored in a retrieval system, or transmitted, in any form or by any means, without the prior permission in writing of the author. Publications are exempt in the case of brief quotations in critical reviews or articles.

Contents

Chapter 1 – Mule (July 269 AD) 1

Chapter 2 – God Tree 12

Chapter 3 – Braduhenna 22

Chapter 4 – Shade 30

Chapter 5 – Coin 39

Chapter 6 – Verona 49

Chapter 7 – Deception 58

Chapter 8 – Mountains 69

Chapter 9 – Via Claudia Augusta 76

Chapter 10 – Black 84

Chapter 11 – Dragon 93

Chapter 12 – Lever 103

Chapter 13 – Parley 113

Chapter 14 – Retreat 122

Chapter 15 – Shore 131

Contents (continued)

Chapter 16 – Tax (August 269 AD) 142

Chapter 17 – Plunder 151

Chapter 18 – Family (October 269 AD) 161

Chapter 19 – Naissus 173

Chapter 20 – Little Wolf 186

Chapter 21 – Equal (December 269 AD) 195

Chapter 22 – Bloodshed 208

Chapter 23 – Tether 216

Chapter 24 – Invaders 225

Chapter 25 – Vandali 233

Chapter 26 – Malady 242

Chapter 27 – Slur (February 270 AD) 253

Chapter 28 – Aquileia (April 270 AD) 264

Chapter 29 – Emperor 275

Chapter 30 – Friend 286

Contents (continued)

Chapter 31 – Dice (May 270 AD) 297

Chapter 32 – Haemus Mountains 305

Chapter 33 – Hannibal 315

Chapter 34 – Camp 323

Chapter 35 – Peace and War (July 270 AD) 334

Historical Note – Main characters 341

Historical Note – Imperator storyline 345

Historical Note – Random items 347

Historical Note – Place names 352

Chapter 1 – Mule (July 269 AD)

The Via Postumia, Northern Italia.

Near the small town of Cadianum, just east of Verona.

Twenty paces beyond the edge of the cobbles, a peasant farmer trudged across a field that shimmered golden in the midday sun. The man's leathered skin gleamed with sweat as he strained against the rough-hewn handles of a two-wheeled harvester. Without warning, the mule that was harnessed to the *vallus* stopped in its tracks, baulking at the toil.

The farmer issued a sigh, wiped the perspiration from his face with the hem of his grimy tunic, and took a long swig from a waterskin.

Then he gripped the wood once more and clicked his tongue to encourage the obstinate beast.

It helped naught.

The man shook his head, issued a string of curses, and eased the heavy contraption to the ground. He plucked a whip from his belt and lashed the rump of the mule. The animal brayed in protest, but obediently plodded on.

As we trotted past, the sweltering heat spawned a dust devil that whirled across a nearby threshing floor, prompting a winnowing slave to drop her woven basket and grab at her shift. The unexpected gust engulfed us in a cloud of fine dust and wheat chafe. Instinctively we spurred our mounts to escape the suffocating haze.

Once we were clear, Gordas reined in and reached for his wineskin. He drank deeply while he watched the labourer and his beast of burden stomp closer. The mule, that appeared as exhausted as its master, was slick with perspiration. The animal's head hung low, its tired eyes shrivelled and sunk into its skull.

Gordas took another swig, glaring at the man with a look of contempt. "The dirt eater is killing the mule", he growled in the tongue of the steppes.

The Hun's hostility came as no surprise, as I knew well enough that my barbarian friend despised those who eked out a living by tilling the earth.

"Maybe they expect a summer storm?" Diocles ventured in an attempt to change the subject, and passed Hostilius a full skin. "That is probably why they are so keen to get the wheat under cover."

Apart from a nod, Hostilius offered no comment. We had all noticed that he had become increasingly sullen over the preceding days, a condition that was out of character for the usually outspoken Primus Pilus.

The peasant cursed again and savagely struck the mule.

Gordas's hand dropped to the haft of his battle-axe.

I shared a look with Diocles and nudged Kasirga off the road. As if my horse knew what was expected of him, he halted five paces in front of the cart, blocking the labourer's way.

The man, who had paid us no heed until then, looked up with a scowl plastered on his grimy face. I could not help but catch a whiff of a rancid stench that hinted that his skin had not seen water or oil in days. He was no doubt about to issue a rebuke, but managed to keep a leash on his tongue when he noticed my appearance. Only a complete fool or dullard would dare to affront a man garbed in the uniform of an imperial legate, a man who commands the legions on behalf of the Roman emperor.

The labourer wiped the scowl from his face and inclined his head in supplication. "Lord", he said.

Without a word I swung down from the saddle, cupped a palm, and proceeded to water the mule - fixing the man with an accusatory glare while the creature thirstily lapped up every drop.

The peasant swallowed and licked his lips, concern etched on his weathered face. "I've owned him since he's been a foal, lord. I look after him really well 'cause he's the only one I've got."

I poured more water into my palm, which made the mule happy, but increased the level of anxiety of its owner.

"It… It's just that we've heard rumours of them Germani pouring through the passes, lord", the peasant stammered. "I've got no other choice but to leave the grapes to rot on the vines, but we're trying to bring the wheat in so we can survive the winter." He gestured at the fields surrounding us. "There won't even be time to cut straw to feed old Lucius here", he added, and patted the neck of the mule. "I'll probably have to butcher him when the first snow comes."

"Have no fear. None will ravage these lands", I said.

A frown creased the peasant's brow, but he wisely kept his counsel.

From around a bend in the road, a mile distant, the standard of Emperor Claudius Gothicus appeared. Behind the fur-cloaked signifer rode the emperor himself, surrounded by mounted praetorians, who, in turn, were followed by a column of black-clad Illyrians, their dark armour and whetted lances glimmering in the sun. Trailing the Illyrians was a seemingly endless column of barbarian cavalry, drafted from the ranks of the Goths and Carpiani in the aftermath of their defeat near Naissus.

"I'll go water my mule at the trough then, lord", the man suggested once he had managed to shut his open maw.

"Good", I replied, and glanced at my savage friend, only to notice that the Hun's fist was still clamped around the haft of his weapon even though his gaze was focused elsewhere.

I guided Kasirga onto the cobbles to speak with Gordas. He used his chin to gesture to the western horizon where a handful of black tendrils spiralled to the heavens. "Trouble", he grunted.

"Should we not wait for reinforcements?" Diocles asked. "In case the Germani are still around."

A look of expectancy settled on Gordas's scarred visage and he reached for his lopsided horn bow.

"They will only set buildings to the torch once they are done looting", I said. "They will be long gone by the time we reach the village."

My words seemed to set Diocles at ease, although I noticed Gordas's face drop as he slipped his strung bow back into its pouch.

Hostilius was still staring straight ahead, his expression resembling that of a paid mourner in a funeral procession. I had been friends with the Primus Pilus for close on thirty years and knew from experience that he wished to be left alone.

* * *

"Because of the baths constructed around the hot springs, Cadianum is a favoured place for travellers to spend the night", Diocles enlightened us as we left the broad Via Postumia and turned off on a smaller cobbled road that led to the settlement.

There were no fortifications surrounding the town. The wall of stone, that in bygone days had kept out Gallic raiders from the north, had long ago been cannibalised in order to expand the town.

Before we entered amongst the structures, my aide paused for a moment to stare at the black smoke still pouring from a handful of buildings. "Used to be a favoured destination", he corrected himself, and followed us along the main thoroughfare.

Gordas, Diocles and I walked our horses into the town square, but Hostilius reined in outside the entrance to a small *domus* that was flanked by a *taberna*. Above the shopfront on the crumbling plaster, a faded fresco depicted a satyr handing a bunch of grapes to Bacchus, an indication that the store had until recently belonged to a wine merchant.

I twisted in the saddle and glanced over my shoulder. Hostilius dismounted and tied the reins of his horse to a vandalised hitching rail. He picked up one of the broken amphorae that littered the pavement and gently placed it back on the counter of the wineshop. With a faraway look in his eyes, he ran an open palm across the veined white marble that was worn smooth from many years of use.

I exchanged a look with Gordas, who shrugged and nudged his horse farther into the town.

Apart from a dog barking somewhere in an alleyway, the settlement appeared to be devoid of life. Although it was to be expected following the raid of a peaceful Roman town by a mob of savage Alemanni, what was surprising was that no corpses littered the streets.

"Where is everybody?" Diocles asked, no doubt sharing my confusion.

"Dead", Gordas replied, which earned him a scowl from my aide.

Notwithstanding the jest, the Hun showed that he shared our suspicions by taking his strung bow into his fist. He reached for his quiver and took two arrows in his draw hand.

For the better part of a third of a watch, Diocles, Gordas and I explored the *insulae*, *tabernae* and the occasional larger *domus*. The broken furnishings and bloodstained floors of the houses and shops indicated that the raid was brutal and violent, yet we came across no bodies.

Eventually we made our way back to our horses. "We had better return to the column", I said, and gained the saddle. "Our scouts reported to the emperor that the Alemanni are still traversing the passes, but the attack on Cadianum is proof that at least one warband has already entered the Po Valley. Marcus needs to know."

"Where is Tribune Proculus?" Diocles asked as he mounted.

Of course, Hostilius and his horse were nowhere to be seen.

In order to cover more ground, each of us went in a different direction in search of the Primus Pilus. Diocles and Gordas combed the back alleys while I continued along the main thoroughfare.

I came across Hostilius on the outskirts of the town, three hundred paces from where the old wall must have been. He was kneeling in the dust beside a fractured stone lying on its side. Out of respect for the dead, I dismounted, dropped Kasirga's reins, and made my way towards him.

Judging by the hoofprints and the shattered memorials it was clear that the raiders had despoiled the cemetery to show their contempt for all things Roman.

I peeked over the Primus Pilus's shoulder, tilted my head, and read the inscription carved into the cracked marble.

"Hostilia Manlia. Beloved Grandmother.

Her grandson commissioned this stone for his ava."

Hostilius's cheeks were wet, and I could not help but notice the marks where his tears had fallen onto the dusty stone.

"I grew up in this town, Domitius", he croaked. "My parents were killed when I was but a babe, so my *ava* took me in although she was old. She used to get up before sunrise and went to bed after midnight to keep food on the table. One morning, a month after my sixteenth birthday, she didn't wake up at all."

He took a moment to gather himself.

"I sold the amphora remaining in the *taberna* to get her this stone", he said. "Then I said my goodbyes and went off to join the legions."

The Primus Pilus leaned forward and pressed both his palms onto the rough marble. "I swear in the name of Mars the Avenger that I will not rest until the men who did this are dead", he hissed through clenched teeth.

He slowly gained his feet and turned to face me. Of the sullen sadness there was no sign and he wore a look of steely determination. "We had better get going Domitius", he said. "The Alemanni aren't going to slit their own throats, now are they?"

Before I could offer a reply, a strange chirping sound reached our ears. The noise carried on the back of a breeze that blew in from the direction of the tree-lined banks of the small river bordering the town.

Hostilius narrowed his eyes. "Never heard that kind of bird before", he said.

"Neither have I", I replied.

Chapter 2 – God Tree

Hostilius and I had hardly mounted when Diocles and Gordas arrived at a trot.

The pair reined in abreast of us.

"Did you find any bodies?" I asked.

Gordas shook his head.

The strange sound repeated itself as a gust of wind whipped up dust from amongst the tombstones.

I slipped the loop of a bowstring over the horn nock, strung my weapon in the saddle, and selected an armour-piercing arrow from my quiver. Gordas took a battle-axe into his fist, Hostilius hefted his boar spear and Diocles drew his cavalry sword.

We spread out in a line and walked our horses towards the riverbank.

Twenty paces from the edge of the undergrowth, Gordas raised a palm. For a span of a hundred heartbeats the Hun scanned the treeline. Birds fluttered in the trees, squirrels scurried up trunks to stash acorns for the winter, and dormice scampered in and out of their nests to feed their young.

The Hun tucked the haft of his battle-axe into his belt. "There's no one near", he said, and clicked his tongue to coax his mare onto a deer path. I followed, with Hostilius and Diocles forming the rearguard.

Fifty paces ahead, Gordas exited into a clearing bordering a cobbling stream. I noticed his mare's ears prick up and issue a nervous nicker. He reined in, but rather than reach for a weapon, his head tilted upward, as if staring at the sky, which of course was hidden from view by the oak canopy. I noticed droplets falling from above, which was confusing because the skies had been clear all day.

I came to a halt beside my savage friend and gently stroked Kasirga's neck in an effort to calm him.

My eyes were still fixed on the canopy when Hostilius and Diocles arrived. They reined in alongside, just in time to witness another gust move through the leaves of the ancient oak that towered over us. Willow bark cordage creaked under the strain of the bodies of townspeople that swung from the branches. Their heads lolled to their chests as if they were trying to hide their opened throats as they slowly twirled about, engaged in a macabre dance of the dead. The braided ropes had eaten into the soft bark, right down to the greenwood, causing the knots to issue an eery chirping sound as the corpses oscillated in the wind.

Blood still trickled from the horrific wounds that the raiders had inflicted upon their victims - red droplets dripping down to the carpet of leaves like rainwater trickling through the canopy.

Diocles reached for his face and wiped a speck of bright red from his brow, issuing a shudder of disgust. Gordas stared at the carnage, his face a mask of stone, while the Primus Pilus's fist was clasped around his amulet, his jaw set in a way that showed that he was more determined than ever to honour the oath he had made on the stone of his *ava*.

"Nothing we can do for them now", Hostilius said, and turned his mount's head towards the deer path. "It will be dark by the time we get back to the column. Come morning, I will send a *turma* to cut them down and give them a decent burial."

I was about to follow the Primus Pilus when my eye caught movement high up in the branches. Gordas must have seen it as well, and in the blink of an eye he had an arrow nocked and his bowstring was at his ear. He glanced in my direction and I replied with a slight shake of my head.

Hostilius must have noticed our silent discourse. He turned his horse around and reined in beside me. I waited for Diocles to approach so that he, too, could hear my words. "Don't look now", I said. "But there is someone, or something, hiding in the tree."

"I played here when I was a boy", Hostilius whispered, and gestured with his head towards the massive trunk of the ancient oak. "Up there's a hollow where I used to hide from my *ava* whenever I got up to mischief." He eyed the bole. "In fact, I'm sure it's still there."

Before I could reply, Hostilius swung down from the saddle. With an ease that was hard to comprehend, he scampered up the trunk like an oversized squirrel.

Thirty feet up, he swung his leg over a thick branch to straddle it. Facing the trunk, he started to talk in a low whisper.

For long the Primus Pilus remained up in the canopy. Eventually he extended his open arms and a small girl, mayhap six or seven years old, emerged from her hiding place and fell into his embrace. Hostilius clasped his left arm around the sobbing child and started to make his way down the trunk, making sure to keep her eyes away from the grisly scene. He mounted without a word and steered his horse onto the animal track.

Diocles twisted in his saddle and leaned in closer. "Do you think her family still lives, legate?" he asked.

"There were only male corpses hanging from the branches", I said. "Her mother and siblings have most probably been taken as slaves."

"I want to go home", I heard the girl sob to Hostilius.

"We will first have to chase the bad men away", the Primus Pilus replied. He allowed her to cry, waiting patiently until the child's curiosity got the better of her grief.

"Who are you?" she asked.

"I am a soldier of Rome who chase away bad people", he said. "My name is Hostilius."

I pulled in beside the Primus Pilus.

"This is Lucius, Gaia. He is a friend", Hostilius said when the little urchin turned her wide eyes on me.

I issued a smile of acknowledgement, which seemed to satisfy the child.

Her eyes flicked to Diocles. "Hello Lady Gaia, I am Diocles", my aide said.

For a moment I believed that the child would start crying when her gaze settled on the Hun, but Hostilius pacified her with his words. "Whenever the Germani see Gordas, they run away."

Gordas offered her a smile and Gaia reciprocated.

The Hun's scarred, tattooed visage and elongated head put the fear of the gods into battle-hardened warriors, but for some reason or other, children seemed to take to him. We had not even reached the Postumian Way when Gaia asked to ride with Gordas. He spoke with her in whispers while she held the reins of his horse, believing that she was directing it, while the Hun steered it with his legs, of course.

Arriving back with the army, Gordas, Hostilius and I helped Gaia to light a fire. On my instruction, Diocles disappeared to procure hot food from the *praetorium*. Once we were seated on furs beside the flames, the Greek returned with a plate stacked with small loaves, grilled chicken and a few rounds of cheese. In his other hand he carried an amphora of honey.

Once the flames had warmed her little body and her tummy bulged with food, I asked her, "Tell us what happened, Gaia."

She sneaked a peek at Gordas, who gave her a little nod. I noticed that her right hand reached underneath her cloak, I assumed to grasp her *lanula*, the moon-shaped amulet Roman girls wore to ward off evil. She closed her eyes for a heartbeat to issue a silent prayer to whomever god she favoured.

"Yesterday evening when my *tata* came home from the *popina* he was very happy. Tata emptied the purse on the table and there were so many silvers", she said, gesturing with her hands to indicate an impossibly large heap of coins.

"He won it in a game of dice because Fortuna likes him", she said, her expression serious. "He promised to buy new shifts for Mama, Clementia and me", she added, and I could see the excitement in her eyes.

"Were you at home when the bad people came, Gaia?" Diocles asked.

"Clementia said that she would make sure that Tata buys me a red shift", she said. "She pulled my hair when I said that I liked blue better."

The little girl's Latin was not the bastardised kind one would expect of a peasant. It made me suspect that her mother's family was of better stock but had fallen onto hard times, an occurrence that was not uncommon in the day and age we lived in.

"What did you do then?" I asked.

"I bit her hand", she replied, "so Mama wasn't very happy with us."

Gaia paused to take a sip from the small cup of honeyed wine that Diocles had mixed for her.

"Mama took a silver from Tata's purse and told me to go to the butcher's shop to buy a joint of smoked pork", she said. "She sent Clementia to the other side of the street to get a dozen loaves."

"Uncle Fabricius gave me a large joint", she said. "It was very heavy."

She took another sip.

"I was walking home when I saw two men in the street", she continued. "They were giants and they had swords in their hands." She indicated men who, to her young eyes, must have appeared eight feet tall.

Gordas wrapped an arm around her trembling shoulders.

"What did you do?" Hostilius asked.

"I tried to run away, but my legs didn't want to listen to me, Uncle Hostilius", she said, and hung her head in shame. "When the giants shouted at me I became so scared that my feet woke up. I ran into an alley between the butcher's shop and the *popina*."

A cook arrived from the praetorium with a plate of sweetmeats that Diocles had arranged earlier. "Minced date and wheat cakes for the little lady", he said, and received a smile from Gaia.

"Did they follow you?" I asked, and held the plate out to the girl.

"They tried to", she said while chewing, and held her palms two feet apart. "But the walls were too close together and the giants had to shuffle sideways."

The recounting of the episode made her break out in tears. "I dropped the joint of pork", she said through the sobs. "And I was too scared to turn back."

"Is that why you hid in the tree?" Gordas asked, stroking the child's hair.

"Yes", she said. "Mama would have wrung my neck if I went home without the pork or the silver."

"Did you see what happened to the villagers, Gaia?" Diocles asked.

"I didn't look, but I think the lady must have hurt them", she said. "Because they screamed a lot." Again, Gaia reached for her amulet to banish the evil thoughts.

"The lady?" I asked.

She nodded and took another sweetmeat from the plate. "The lady that sat on the black horse told the giants what to do", Gaia said. "The lady on the horse is very pretty but she has an ugly voice."

"Do you remember her name?" Hostilius asked while Gaia took the last swallow from her cup.

"The giants called her Braduhenna", Gaia said, yawned, and lay down with her head on Gordas's lap.

Chapter 3 – Braduhenna

While we waited at the flap, Gordas gently laid Gaia down on the furs inside the tent and retreated with stealth. He paused at the doorway to fix the guard with a glare that left no doubt in either of their minds what the consequences would be if anything untoward were to befall the little girl.

After Hostilius issued a grunt, which I construed as being in support of Gordas, we made our way to the headquarters tent.

"Who is this woman that you have sworn to kill, centurion?" Marcus asked once we had told him of the day's happenings.

"Just another barbarian witch", Hostilius sighed. "If I'm not mistaken, she was the one who poisoned the Alemanni king's mind against Rome when we were stationed at Mogantiacum in Germania?"

The duty tribune pushed aside the flap. "Lord Emperor", he said. "The Frank has arrived."

"Show him in", Marcus commanded.

The tribune issued a nod and bade the visitor to enter. Moments later, a hulking warrior ducked through the doorway and inclined his head to Marcus. "Lord Emperor, you wished to speak with me?"

Marcus indicated for Hlodwig to take a seat. "Tell us about the one called Braduhenna", he said.

The big Frank visibly stiffened at the mention of the name. "She is the war matron of the Alemanni", he said. His gazed settled on me before he added, "Some say that she communes with Teiwaz."

"I tried to find information about the Alemanni in the scrolls", Diocles said. "The first cursory reference to the tribe was about sixty years ago. How come they managed to gain so much power in such a short time?"

Hlodwig took a long swig from his cup. "In the time of my grandfather, they were a people of little consequence - no more than an irritation in the eyes of the larger tribes", he said. "In those days, the formidable Chatti wished to conquer their lands. The Alemanni trembled with fear and sent a messenger to Emperor Caracalla pleading for his help."

Diocles issued a nod. "They are first mentioned in the time of Caracalla", he confirmed. "The emperor marched to their assistance, but the Alemanni treacherously attacked the legions when they crossed the Rhine."

Hlodwig eyed Diocles with amusement. "Who drew the letters on your scrolls, Roman?" he asked.

"The scribes of the emperor, of course", Diocles replied.

"Then the vellum the words are written on is of little more use other than to start a cooking fire", Hlodwig said. "The Franks hate the Alemanni even more than they despise Rome", he said. "Despite this, my grandfather told me the truth of what happened in the days of Emperor Caracalla. In fact, all north of the river know of Rome's treachery."

"The emperor answered the pleas of the Alemanni and he and his legions were welcomed in the lands across the Rhine", Hlodwig said, using a sweeping gesture to indicate the hinterland. "The people of the tribe lined the roads and cheered their iron-clad saviours as they marched. The war leader arranged a feast to welcome his Roman allies, but when the warriors of the tribe were drunk on mead, your emperor ordered his legions to slaughter them. A handful escaped and sought the counsel of the woman of their murdered war leader."

"She suggested the unimaginable and persuaded them to accompany her to the lands of the very men who were planning on exterminating the Alemanni. The Chatti war chief was as impressed by the courage of Braduhenna as he was incensed by the actions of Caracalla. He called upon the tribes that owed them allegiance. The Bucinobantes, Hermanduri, Mattiaci, Narisci and even the obstinate Nemetes answered the call and joined their brethren on a quest for revenge."

"The allied tribes marched to the lands of the Alemanni and met Caracalla's legions on the battlefield", Hlodwig said, and took another swig to wet his throat.

"That", Diocles said, "is recorded in the scrolls. Caracalla was victorious and ended up making peace with the Germani."

Hlodwig issued a guffaw. "Why would a king who wins a battle pay the beaten enemy ten wagonloads of gold coin?" he asked.

Diocles shrugged. "Probably because the Germani won, but Caracalla wished for the rabble back in Rome to think otherwise."

"My grandsire stood in the ranks of the allied army", Hlodwig said proudly. "He told of how Rome's Eastern bowmen darkened the sky with shafts. With his own eyes he witnessed Germani warriors, their courage inflamed by the words and prayers of Braduhenna, pluck arrows from their limbs with their teeth so they could slay their foes without pause."

"I've seen their kind do that", Hostilius confirmed. "If you want to take on those big brutes, you'd better know your business."

The Primus Pilus's words pleased Hlodwig, who nodded and continued. "The battle raged all day. Eventually, after the sun had set, the Romans retreated to their camp to lick their wounds. The following morning, the emperor sent an envoy to buy peace with gold."

"I am surprised that the Germani accepted", I said. "When their honour is insulted, only the blood of the enemy will wash away the stain."

Hlodwig nodded. "Despite her hatred for Rome, Braduhenna was the one who convinced the war chiefs to accept the bribe", he said. "In the aftermath of the battle, she made peace with the Chatti and used her share of the tribute not for herself, but to buy the goodwill of the other, smaller tribes. In the months that followed, when one of the allies was attacked, the Alemanni rushed to their aid and fought at their side to gain revenge for their brothers. Soon the six tribes of the Alemanni were bound by blood and honour."

"It is said that Braduhenna lives in a holy grove deep in the dark forest where she communes with the gods", Hlodwig added reverently. "The few who have laid eyes on her swear that she has not aged a day since she unified the tribes."

"In fact", he added, "there are some who believe that the war matron is even older - that she was born in the time of your Caesar Augustus. They say that Braduhenna was the one who whispered into the ear of Arminius who destroyed Rome's legions in the forests of Germania all those years ago."

I saw that Hostilius was about to voice his thoughts, which, if they were what I expected them to be, would have been construed as an insult by the Frank.

Before the words left the Primus Pilus's mouth, I raised an open palm. "Thank you Hlodwig", I said. "You have enlightened us. I can see why you are valued by your lord, Haldagates."

"Hlodwig's version of Caracalla's campaign against the Germani is probably accurate", Marcus said once the Frank was out of earshot.

"It is plausible", Diocles replied. "Some believe that subsequent to arranging the murder of his brother, Geta, Caracalla went on campaign just to bolster his image in the eyes of the rabble back in Rome. After he paid off the barbarians to gain a victory, he improved the fortifications along the Rhine. Why would he have done that if he had crushed the enemy?"

Hostilius took a swig from his cup. "I wouldn't be surprised if the Germani kicked Caracalla's arse because he was a pompous, good-for-nothing pansy", Hostilius said. "But how, in the name of the gods, can Braduhenna still be running around the countryside with the savages? She must be at least eighty years old."

"It appears as if the Germani believe that the gods have bestowed upon Braduhenna the gift of eternal youth", I said.

"It is not uncommon for sibyls to create the illusion of longevity", Diocles asserted. "Greek oracles who lived in relative seclusion have tricked the populace into believing that they were somehow immune to the ravages of time by substituting themselves with an acolyte or a daughter. The practice of Germani priestesses are probably no different."

Hostilius reached for his amulet. "One can never be sure with these savages", he said. "Who knows which dark gods that witch communes with."

"If their war matron accompanies them, the barbarians will fight like men possessed", I said.

"Whomever or whatever she is won't change the oath I've made on the stone of my *ava*", Hostilius growled. He slowly rotated his cup, his eyes focused on the wine. "She and her warband will have to die."

"There is a practical problem though, tribune", Diocles said, addressing Hostilius. "According to Haldagates the invaders number close on fifty thousand. How will you know which ones despoiled the final resting place of your grandmother?"

It was clear that my aide's words irked Hostilius. "If you're so clever, why don't you tell me how?" the Primus Pilus replied.

Suddenly all eyes were on Diocles, who raised his shoulders in a shrug. "Theoretically, one solution would be to kill them all", he jested. "That way, you will be sure to honour your oath."

For long Hostilius stared into his cup, thinking on my aide's words.

"Not a bad suggestion, Greek", Hostilius eventually said. "I concede - let's do it your way."

Chapter 4 – Shade

When I exited my tent the following morning, I found Gaia with Hostilius and Gordas, diligently helping them prepare flatbread to break our fast.

"Uncle Hostilius says that he will try to find my mama and *tata*", Gaia said. "Are you going to help him and Uncle Gordas look for them?"

"Of course I will, Gaia", I replied, and she smiled broadly in reply.

I was unsure about what to do with the child. We could certainly not put her life in danger by taking her into battle, but neither did I feel comfortable leaving her in the care of strangers.

It was Hostilius who provided the answer. "Gaia tells me that her mother's sister lives in Verona", he said.

"And my uncle is a very important man", the girl added. "He writes letters for the magistrate of the city."

Diocles arrived just then. "Is he a scribe?" my aide asked.

"I've heard Mama call him that", she said. "But Tata calls him a pompous…" She clasped her hand over her mouth to stop her from uttering the word. "I don't think my *tata* likes him. It's because my uncle believes he is better than us."

"Can we leave you with your aunt and uncle while we go look for your mama and papa?" I asked.

Gaia's expression turned serious. "I want to help find my mama and *tata*", she said.

"Someone must stay in Verona if your parents come looking for you, Gaia", Hostilius said. "So you will be helping by staying with your aunt."

His words placated the child and she issued a nod.

"Can we trust these people?" the Primus Pilus asked in the tongue of the Sea of Grass just after Gordas and Gaia left to collect the horses.

I noticed Marcus approaching, surrounded by his guards. "Better prepare a scroll that will explain what is required of them", I suggested to Diocles. "Maybe I can persuade the emperor to put his seal to it."

* * *

A large host, even if composed only of cavalry, inevitably covers less ground than a handful of riders. It was for this reason that Hostilius, Gordas, Diocles and I decided to leave our pack animals with the column and ride ahead to Verona.

When I informed Marcus, he nodded his approval although he failed to suppress a scowl. "I would prefer to accompany you", he said as he pressed his seal ring onto the hot bitumen before ruffling Gaia's hair. "But decorum demands that I lead the army."

"To hades with being proper", Hostilius replied, and offered the emperor his spare *sagum*. "Nobody will give a rotten fig about decorum after we crush the Germani."

Marcus grinned at the Primus Pilus's words, passed the scroll back to Diocles, and accepted the hooded cloak. "I suppose you are right, tribune", he said.

"Of course I'm right", Hostilius replied as he swung up into the saddle.

* * *

Diocles volunteered to remain with the army to ensure that our belongings were loaded and that the emperor's orders were adhered to.

The sun was less than a handspan above the eastern horizon when Marcus, Hostilius, Gordas and I rode from camp. Gaia, of course, insisted on sharing Gordas's saddle.

Just outside Cadianum we passed a marker which indicated that the city of Verona was twelve miles away.

"Descending from the Brenner Pass, Verona is the gateway to the Po Valley and the riches of Italia", Marcus said when he noticed the stone. "I have sent orders ahead to the magistrate to prepare for a siege."

"If I recall correctly, Emperor Gallienus had the city walls strengthened a few years ago", I said.

The Primus Pilus had never cared for Marcus's predecessor, who, in his eyes, had been a pampered aristocrat. "He was good at hiding behind walls", Hostilius said with a smirk.

"The Alemanni will attempt to breach the walls and cross the river", I replied.

"Why not destroy the bridge?" Gordas asked.

"The walls not only guard the bridge", I said. "It also encloses an ancient ford in the river. Even if we destroyed the bridge across the Athesis, they would still be able to cross the river if they breach the walls. If we can stop the invaders before the walls of Verona they will be forced to go home or make their way across the swamps."

Although it was only the first watch of the day, the sun already beat down relentlessly, roasting us inside our armour. As the morning progressed, the thin breeze died away and the dust that it had raised from the fields hung thick in the air.

We were less than halfway to Verona when Gordas reined in near where a minor road branched off to the left. He scanned the countryside, his gaze settling on a dilapidated farmhouse beside a lone ash tree. "Is this the place?" the Hun asked while patting the sweat-slick neck of his mare.

Gaia issued a nod. "The river is close to the road", she said. "Tata waters the mules there whenever we go to the city."

Marcus guided his horse off the main road. "We might as well reconnoitre the Athesis", he jested, and wiped the perspiration from his brow with a forearm. "We can sit in the shade while we suck on our wineskins and watch out for the enemy."

Two hundred heartbeats later, Hostilius dismounted in the shade of the poplars and oaks lining the northern bank of the river. He dropped the reins to allow his horse to drink before he crouched down and scooped a helmet of cold water, which he emptied over his head. "That's better", he said as he flopped down onto the thick grass and lay down flat on his back. "I haven't been this hot since we trudged across those godforsaken deserts in Parthia."

Marcus and I followed Hostilius's example while Gordas loitered in the vicinity of the horses.

"It is good to be away from the eyes of others", Marcus said after a while. "It feels like the good times when we spent our days hunting in the hills north of Sirmium." He issued a sardonic guffaw. "What I wouldn't have given to be the emperor of Rome thirty years ago."

Above us in the canopy, birds chirped and squirrels scurried about. It was hard to believe that not far away, a horde of savages was approaching through the passes.

"Where is Gaia?" Hostilius asked as he raised himself onto his elbows.

The Primus Pilus's question killed the conversation. I immediately noticed that not only was Gaia nowhere to be seen, but the birds, that until moments before were chirping happily, had also gone silent.

I jumped up into a crouch, my hand finding the hilt of my blade. Marcus and Hostilius followed suit. Gordas, who still stood in the shallows with the horses, took a battle-axe into his fist.

A twig snapped somewhere farther up the bank, and three heartbeats later a figure stepped from the underbrush. A chill went down my spine when I laid eyes on the woman. There was little doubt in my mind who it was.

She was the spitting image of Gaia, only older - as if the girl that we had last seen moments before had aged thirty years in three hundred heartbeats. Braduhenna was strikingly beautiful, tall, well-proportioned, and held herself with confidence. Her raven black hair accentuated her pale blue eyes and milk white skin. She wore a dark green shift of woven wool and her hair was braided in the style of the Germani. It was what hung around her neck that turned my stomach - a necklace of sculpted gold discs.

Hostilius must have noticed it as well. "By the gods", he said. "Those are *phalerae* issued for bravery, the kind that senior centurions wear." Then his eyes went wide and he turned as white as a bleached tunic. "Look, Domitius", he whispered.

"It's the goat, boar and lion of Varus's legions that met their fate in the dark forests of Germania."

The woman reached up and stroked the gold discs with slender fingers. "Beautiful, isn't it", she said in perfect Latin. "I collected them myself after our warriors defeated the iron legions", she added, issuing a dazzling smile that displayed her perfect teeth.

Just then there was a rustle of leaves and Gaia appeared beside the woman, confirming my suspicion that she was a younger version of the Germani lady. "We didn't kill all the Romans", Braduhenna said, as if divining our thoughts. "We only sacrificed the officers. I took a few of the scribes as my personal slaves. Besides cleaning pigsties, they excelled at teaching me your horrid tongue."

We were still too overawed to speak, staring at the apparition with open mouths.

Braduhenna reached out and placed an arm around Gaia's shoulders. "Thank you for taking care of my daughter, Romans", she said. She pulled the child closer and gently kissed her hair. "You did well, my darling."

Gaia, or whatever the wicked little thing's name was, glared at us with cold eyes devoid of emotion. A humourless smile, which I found extremely unsettling, split her thin lips.

"Thank you Mama, it was easy", she said in her native tongue. "And you were right, they stink of horse."

Chapter 5 – Coin

Gaia pointed her finger at me. "That one is the war leader of the Romans, mama", she said. "The short, fat one beside him is his oathsworn warrior."

I heard Hostilius issue a low, guttural growl at the insult, and prayed that he would be able to restrain himself.

She indicated Gordas. "So is the ugly one."

The warriors of the Eastern Steppes pride themselves in their ability to intimidate with their appearance, and the girl's words brought an expression of satisfaction to the Hun's scarred visage.

"Who is he?" Braduhenna asked and gestured at Marcus.

Gaia shrugged in reply. "I think he is a scribe."

I silently thanked the gods that the girl was not aware of the fact that Marcus was the emperor of Rome. Fortuna must have favoured us and the war matron's gaze settled on me instead.

"I have heard the name of Eochar the Merciless whispered around the campfires of my warriors", Braduhenna said, a frown of amusement on her brow. "They say that you are a Scythian who walks in the shadow of Teiwaz."

For a heartbeat I expected Braduhenna to reach for a blade, but it was not the way of Germani women. She raised a hand and a dozen spear fighters stepped from the shadows of the trees. They were undoubtedly handpicked to guard the lady of the Alemanni.

Our shields and bows were strapped to our saddles and I knew that we would not prevail against men who could wield their weapons from a distance.

The gods intervened. Which ones, I do not know, but I would like to believe that it was the war god who wished to be entertained.

"I need them alive for the ritual", Braduhenna commanded her ringmen. "It matters not if they are wounded." She turned to face us. "Lay down your blades and I will be merciful. Your deaths will be quick."

I doubted whether the witch fully comprehended the meaning of the word. I was not willing to confirm my suspicion, so I slipped my sword from the scabbard and took a step towards the nearest spearman.

There is almost always at least one man in a group who wishes to distinguish himself from his peers. It was no different with the oathsworn of Braduhenna. A short, stocky warrior with a bull-like neck rushed at me. He brandished a spear, intent on being the one to claim the honour of besting a legend.

Nowadays warriors frown upon the spear as an outdated tool, one preferred by peasants and barbarians. Graveyards are full of men who underestimated the father of weapons. The legions had long ago abandoned the spear in favour of the gladius, but only because the shortsword is more effective when wielded at close quarters. Did Alexander of Macedon not conquer the Persians with the spear? Did the famed Greek hero, Achilles, not prefer it to the sword?

I waited until the last moment before I twisted my body to the side to avoid the leaf-shaped iron tip that the attacker thrust at my stomach. When the whetted head brushed past the scales of my armour, I struck with the speed of an adder. My fist clamped around the attacker's spear, just behind the iron, allowing me a fraction of a heartbeat for the edge of my blade to whip along the haft of his weapon, peeling his fingers from the wood like a kitchen wench slicing carrots.

Horrified, he relinquished his weapon in favour of gripping the stumps of his bleeding appendages. I caught the proffered spear with my left hand just before the edge of my blade opened his jugular.

Somehow I managed to duck beneath the swipe of the warrior behind him, and pierced the man's neck with an underhand thrust from my borrowed weapon. The third man was cautious and jabbed at me, his weight on his back foot. The steel of my blade cut the tip from the haft of his spear. He stumbled backwards and fell over his own feet in his eagerness to avoid my sword, which I plunged into his torso as I stepped over the corpse.

From the corner of my eye, I spied Hostilius strike down a foe. He issued a feral roar and bodily charged into two warriors who were simultaneously assailing Marcus.

I heard the swoosh of Gordas's battle-axe and another of Braduhenna's oathsworn stumbled into my field of vision. The wounded man clutched at the Hun's blade, embedded deep in his cheek. The brute facing me eyed his dying comrade. When he turned his head in my direction, my borrowed spear was already cutting a path through the air, fishtailing under the power of my cast. The iron tip sliced through his mail armour and lodged deep in his chest.

I plucked the blade from the body and suddenly there were no more warriors who barred the way to Braduhenna. I hefted the spear, but before I could rid the world of the witch, she took the child in her arms, using the girl as a shield.

Simultaneously she issued a wail that would have made a siren proud.

I heard the rustle of men running through the forest and assumed that she had called for reinforcements. "Kill them all. Kill them all", she screeched, no doubt having decided to settle on alternative offerings to her god. "I swear by all the gods of Germania that I will kill you, Eochar the Merciless! You are a dead man!"

At least a dozen more warriors ran from the shadows. Three swarmed around Braduhenna. Two of them approached me, while the third whisked the war matron and her daughter to safety. She shrugged off her rescuer's arm and her gaze met mine. When she spoke, her voice was calm and her eyes cold. "You might escape today, Roman", she said. "But your fate is sealed. The oracles and seers north of the Mother River have prophesied that the Battle of the Dark Wood will be played out again. You see, Roman, you and your men will suffer the same fate as Varus and his legions."

At that moment, both the foes charged.

I blocked the thrust of the first warrior and managed to avoid a quick series of jabs from the other, but my foot caught in a rabbit hole as I stepped back and I ended up stumbling onto a knee. Sensing that I was vulnerable, the two Germani moved in for the kill.

Having lost my balance, I was unable to position myself to repel their onslaught. Sizing up the warriors in a heartbeat, I decided to eliminate the threat on the left, gambling that my armour would save me from the first strike of the second oathsworn. From bended knee, I lunged forward with my spear, forcing the target of my attack to raise his shield. It was a feint, and I sliced low with my sword to cut into his shin. My weapon cleft only air as the Germani, who possessed catlike reflexes, sprang back. In that moment the other warrior struck with a swipe at my torso. The powerful strike toppled me onto my back and I heard the ripping sound as the iron blade tore scales from my armour.

Both ringmen moved to attack while I was down. Inexplicably, they hesitated. I heard footfalls behind me and, assuming the worst, jumped to my feet. I swung around and raised my blade in an attempt to block the expected strike. Instead of encountering a foe, I came face to face with Hlodwig and Diocles. At that moment the giant Frank cast his *francisca*. The oathsworn who had tried to stab me in the back raised his shield, but the heavy throwing axe from the hand of the giant warrior shattered the wood, sliced through mail, and thudded into his chest, accompanied by a sound akin to a butcher chopping through the ribcage of a bovine carcass. The other attacker turned tail and vanished into the woods.

We were still outnumbered, but the brief pause had provided Gordas with the opportunity to get a string to his bow. I heard successive whooshes, and armour-piercing arrows sprouted from the faces of the two men nearest to the Hun.

The Germani were given a brief respite as Gordas identified his targets. Thrice he drew back the string and the warriors surrounding Marcus fell to the wayside, clutching bloodied shafts protruding from their necks.

I rushed to Kasirga and before the attackers could regroup, my Hun bow was in my fist and four arrows in my draw hand.

* * *

Hostilius turned over another Alemanni corpse with his booted foot. "I think this is the last one", he shouted from the edge of the clearing. "That makes it thirty-two."

"Thirty-three", Diocles replied from within the thicket along the riverbank and dragged another body into the light.

"How did you know there would be trouble?" Marcus asked Diocles once my aide had dumped the corpse.

Diocles turned to where the hulking Frank was stripping the dead of armbands and trinkets. "Show the emperor", Diocles said.

Hlodwig rummaged through his purse that bulged with coin looted from the corpses. Eventually he produced a leather thong with a gold coin attached. He bowed his head in respect and presented it to Marcus. "Lord Diocles found this amongst the furs where the little girl slept", the Frank said.

Marcus studied the coin, flipped it in his hand, and passed it to me. The image of Augustus Caesar was still crisp and detailed. The reverse side was worn smooth from rubbing against skin. What drew my attention was the strange symbol crudely etched into the metal.

Hlodwig noticed my interest. "It is the mark of Vihansa, the goddess of the field of spears", he said. "Lord Diocles said that the child reached for it many times. Only an acolyte of a war priestess would wear such a powerful symbol against her heart."

"It was clear that the child is not who she claimed to be", Diocles explained, "so I had Hlodwig track you."

Hostilius slapped Diocles's back. "Not bad for a Greek", the Primus Pilus said.

My aide smiled at the compliment and gestured at the pierced coin in my hand. "What is interesting, though, is that the coin was minted just before the Varian disaster in the forests of Germania", he said. "It must have been looted from the body of a dead legionary."

The mention of Varus jogged Marcus's memory. "I remember that the witch said something about Varus?" he remarked.

"She said that their oracles foretold that the Varian disaster will repeat itself", I said.

Hostilius issued a guffaw. "That will never happen", he said. "I wouldn't waste my time to discuss the drivel that comes from that evil bitch's lips."

I noticed that Hlodwig lowered his gaze. The big man suddenly appeared markedly uncomfortable.

"What have you heard north of the River?" I asked the Frank.

"The seers speak of it", he said. "They say that they heard the whispers of the old gods in the ancient groves."

"What do they say?" Marcus asked, a frown creasing his brow.

"They say that the Battle of the Dark Wood will play itself out again, lord", Hlodwig replied reverently.

And then the god of the field of blood whispered into my ear.

Chapter 6 – Verona

Later that same day, Marcus invited us to dine with him at the imperial residence in Verona. Years before, Gallienus had revamped the palace. The previous emperor had frequently travelled to Germania during the time that he ruled jointly with his father, Valerian. The exclusive villa, that had remained fully staffed, functioned as a halfway house between Rome and the Rhine frontier, enabling the emperor to rest and recuperate after many hours in a coach or litter.

"To Emperor Gallienus", Hostilius said, and raised his cup of *falernian* against the backdrop of the setting sun.

We reciprocated.

"The main army of the Alemanni is still days from entering Italia", Marcus said, took a sip from his cup, and passed around a bowl of dates. "We need to decide on a strategy to defeat the invaders."

I popped one of the sweet fruits into my mouth, followed by a handful of roasted almonds.

"I cannot deny that I am slightly concerned about the prophecies", Diocles said. "Although I agree with Tribune

Hostilius that the witch's words should be discarded as the drivel it probably is."

Hostilius issued a grunt and leaned forward to dip a small, fresh-baked loaf into a bowl of honey. "Braduhenna's words don't seem to bother you in the least, Domitius", he said while chewing. "I wonder why?"

I swallowed down the dates and nuts with a mouthful of *basarangian* which, if the inscription on the amphora could be believed, had been looted from the cellars of Ctesiphon by Septimius Severus almost a hundred years before. "The priests and priestesses of the Germani are not to be taken lightly", I said. "Like the seers and oracles of Roman lands, they, too, are close to the gods."

Hostilius narrowed his eyes. "So exactly what are you saying, Domitius?" he asked while he dipped another loaf in olive oil. "Are you implying that we will have our arses kicked?"

I took a moment to consider my response. "I believe that the barbarian seers are correct", I said. "And no, Rome will not suffer a repeat of the Varian disaster."

My words brought frowns to all present on the airy colonnaded balcony.

I bit into a ripe fig and broke off a piece of soft cheese from a round to complement the sweet fruit.

"For the sake of the gods, spit it out", Hostilius said.

"Braduhenna assumes that a repeat of the Battle of the Dark Wood means that the Roman forces will suffer a defeat, like they did all those years ago in the time of Augustus", I said, and took a sip to wet my throat. "What if, this time around, the Germani were to be ambushed by Rome, and defeated? Would that not be a repeat of the famous battle?"

A sly smile split Marcus's lips. "It certainly would", he replied.

"The Alemanni are traversing territory that we know well, but they are unfamiliar with", Diocles mused. "And the terrain certainly lends itself to an ambush."

"Tell us what you have in mind, Lucius", Marcus said.

I did as my emperor commanded.

* * *

Diocles weighted down the *itinerarium* with our empty cups before he pressed a forefinger onto the vellum. "The enemy should arrive in Pons Drusi the day after tomorrow", he said.

Hostilius leaned forward, squinting at the map of the Brenner Pass. "I'm not an owl that can see in the dark, Greek", he chastised my aide.

Diocles sighed and moved the oil lamp closer before he traced his finger from north to south along the Via Claudia Augusta. "Tridentum is about forty-five miles south of Drusus's Bridge."

"The barbarians' advance will be slow due to their heavy wagons", I said. "Their oxen will be tired and hungry after weeks in the passes. I would be surprised if they manage to advance more than twelve miles a day."

"We need to strike at their marching column while they are spread out along the Athesis Valley", Marcus suggested.

Hostilius indicated the high peaks surrounding the river valley. "The valley pass is boxed in by mountains", he said. "We won't be able to get near the savages, never mind ambush them."

Diocles indicated a road to the north and east of Verona. "The Claudia Augusta Altinate connects Tridentum to the East

Coast of Italia", he said, and tapped a finger on the map which told me that he was calculating distances in his head. "To intercept them, we will have to travel one hundred and fifty miles."

I shrugged. "We have horses, don't we?"

"We have an army of dirt eaters who can barely ride", Gordas said, his lips curling up in disgust.

"Not all of them are Goths", I replied. "Five thousand are Carpiani horse archers and almost two thousand are Alani."

"Are you suggesting that we attack the Alemanni with seven thousand men?" Marcus asked.

"No", I replied. "I was thinking of taking a thousand."

My utterance was met by frowns all around.

I raised a palm to stall the questions. "Do not be concerned. I will only poke the bear, not fight it", I said, and explained my plan.

When all were leaving to retire to their furs, Marcus signalled for me to remain. "You are taking a great risk, Lucius", he said. "We could make a stand at Verona and prevent the barbarians from crossing the Athesis into the Po Valley. Sure, they will raid the area north of the river, but they will tire of throwing themselves against the impregnable walls. Soon they will return whence they came."

"If we cower behind walls, Marcus, you will never achieve your ultimate goal", I replied.

For a moment my friend stared back at me, his expression incredulous. Marcus averted his eyes and said, "Do you really believe it is achievable?"

"No manner of fortifications will deter the tribes that dwell north of the Danube", I said. "Only when their fear of Rome exceeds their greed and envy will they stop raiding Roman lands. It will not be enough to only defeat them. I want the handful of survivors to concoct terrible tales of the fate of their sword brothers whose bleached bones litter the valleys of Italia."

"If we do not put the fear of the gods into the tribes, they will come for us, one after the other", I said. "Today it is the Alemanni. Tomorrow it might well be the Marcomanni or mayhap the Semnones."

* * *

Early the following morning, a third of a watch before sunrise, I found Gordas, Hostilius and Diocles in the stables where they were readying their horses. A groomsman stood two paces from the door of Kasirga's stall, nervously eyeing the large stallion whose ears were pinned back against its massive head, the whites of his eyes clearly visible. Just as the servant's hand touched the low door, my horse lashed out and struck the oak planks with such force that the whole structure seemed to shudder.

I noticed that Gordas was discreetly watching from the stall across the passage, a smile playing around the corners of his mouth. The Hun, being one of the few people my stallion allowed near him, was revelling in the groomsman's discomfort.

"The enemy scouts are watching Verona", I said to my friends as I took the saddle from the arms of the stable hand.

"Th... thank you, lord", the man stammered, and hurried away to tend to a less dangerous task.

"Do not underestimate the cunning of the Germani, they are a resourceful people", I said. "The war leaders of the Alemanni will know we command a force of twenty-five thousand horsemen."

"They may be clever, but have not faced the Goths and the Carpiani on the field of battle", Hostilius said while he checked the tack of his gelding.

"Are you concerned that the enemy scouts will notice when a thousand horsemen gallop east?" Diocles asked. "And that they will surmise that we will attempt to ambush their column somewhere in the Brenner Pass?"

"On the contrary", I replied. "I am concerned that they will not see us depart."

"Stop talking in riddles like an oracle, Domitius", Hostilius snapped.

"I want the other side to believe that the bulk of our army has left Verona", I said as I swung up into the saddle and directed my horse towards the gate of the imperial complex.

We refrained from discussing our plans as we walked our horses down the main street of Verona. Just before arriving at the theatre, we turned left, heading towards the Porta Organa Antica, the gate in the eastern wall of the city that gave access to the Postumian Way. Noticing our approach, the duty centurion saluted and the heavy gates swung open.

Outside the wall, twenty thousand barbarian riders were waiting. Aldara, the leader of the Goth cavalry, detached from the column of horsemen and approached at a walk. "Lord Eochar", he said, and inclined his head. "We are ready to ride."

"We will lead the way", I replied, and nudged Kasirga to a trot.

"I thought you said you will be taking only a thousand men with you", Hostilius said, "not the whole bloody army."

"The Illyrians will remain with Marcus", I replied. "But I want the enemy scouts to report that the bulk of our force has ridden east."

Chapter 7 – Deception

"All war is based on deception", I said, quoting the words of Cai. "The Alemanni know that we are on our way, so they will expect our cavalry to ambush their column. Their scouts who reconnoitre the passes will be aware that there is only one road wide enough along which a large force of horsemen can attack."

"The Claudia Augusta Altinate that crosses the path of the barbarians at Tridentum", Diocles divined.

I nodded. "Once they have passed Tridentum, the enemy will expect an ambush from behind. They will place their best warriors at the rear of the column and their less experienced men with the vulnerable baggage train in the centre."

Gordas grinned like a wolf. "And you are suggesting that we strike at their soft underbelly?" he asked. "When and where they least expect it."

"In accordance with the prophecies of their oracles", I replied. "We do not want to disappoint Braduhenna, eh?"

"You do know that south of Tridentum the road is surrounded by peaks that cannot be navigated?" Hostilius remarked.

"Only madmen and mountain goats venture onto those treacherous tracks."

"I doubt whether we will find a madman willing to guide us", I said with a grin. "But I am confident that we could bribe a goatherd."

I am sure that my words of hubris reached the ears of the gods.

* * *

We approached Vicetia at dusk. The evening before, Marcus had sent a courier bearing urgent orders to the magistrate of the city forewarning him of our imminent arrival.

As we were expected, it came as no surprise when a welcoming party met us outside the city. The magistrate was a dour individual who was not at all happy with the prospect of feeding twenty thousand men and arranging grazing for an even greater number of horses.

"We are not a rich city", he said with a scowl, while pointing to the east. "Why not camp outside the walls of Patavium instead? It is the wealthiest city in all of Italia and only twenty miles from here."

I gestured in the opposite direction. "Thirty miles to the west, close on sixty thousand Germani are swarming south along the Via Claudia Augusta", I replied, and indicated the city that had long before outgrown its crumbling wall. "In less than a week the barbarian army will arrive at Vicetia. The only thing that stands between the city and blackened ruins are these men you call savages."

The magistrate's eyes washed over the endless column of Goth and Scythian horsemen. "I guess that one has to make sacrifices for the benefit of the fatherland", he eventually said. "How long will you be staying, legate?"

"I am leaving tonight", I said, and gestured for Aldara to join me. "The *foederati* will remain here until either they, or the enemy, has been vanquished."

The commander of the barbarians walked his horse closer.

"Aldara, this is the headman of the village", I said to the Goth, indicating the magistrate. "He has been tasked by the emperor to provide your warriors with food and wine."

"Thank you, lord", Aldara replied, and issued what I suspected was his attempt at a smile.

"Why is the savage leering at me?" the magistrate asked.

"He requested permission to flay you alive in the event that his men do not receive sufficient rations", I said.

"Surely you did not grant his request?" the magistrate asked, his brow furrowed with concern.

"I am convinced that you do not wish to find out", I replied, and directed Kasirga towards the ranks of Goths that were already moving to set up camp.

"How will I communicate with the barbarian?" he pleaded as I trotted off. "I do not speak their tongue."

I twisted in the saddle. "Find a Goth slave", I suggested. "There will be at least one inside the walls."

* * *

While the commanders of the Carpiani army selected the men that would accompany us, I called Aldara aside. "Tomorrow, just after sunrise, I want you to send three thousand riders north to a place called Tridentum", I said. "The city lies on the route of the invaders and they would have passed there by now. The road south of Tridentum follows a valley hemmed in by mountains. Pursue the enemy into the valley."

"I will issue orders to the headman of the city", I added. "He will gladly provide you with horsemen who are able to guide you along the Roman roads."

My words brought a frown to the Goth commander's brow.

"The Germani is expecting an attack from the rear", I explained. "Their scouts have seen us ride east and would have reported it to their war chiefs. They will be waiting for us."

"I will select the bravest of my men for the mission, Lord Eochar, and I will lead them myself", he said, inclining his head. "We will kill many, even if we all have to perish in the battle."

"No", I replied. "I want you to choose the most cautious of your men. Men who are least inclined to fight. My man, Hlodwig, will lead them. Few know the ways of the Germani better than him."

Another frown of confusion creased the Goth commander's brow.

"I want the three thousand riders to harry the rear of their column", I explained. "They are to retreat whenever the enemy tries to engage. When night falls and they make camp, each man must light his own fire. The foe's scouts will report that the entire Goth force is pursuing them."

A wolfish grin split the bearded face of Aldara. "I will make sure that the Germani never know the true numbers of the three thousand", he said. "We will hunt their scouts and strike like the jackal who flees when the wolf bares its teeth."

"Good", I said. "Keep the rest of your men ready. I will need them when I return."

* * *

We left nineteen thousand barbarian horsemen and an irate magistrate outside the walls of Vicetia, on the banks of the Little Medoacus.

We were too deep in friendly territory to be seen by an enemy scout, but erring on the side of caution, we departed a third of a watch after nightfall. Riding in our wake were a thousand Carpiani archers, all mounted on the hardy horses favoured by the tribes of the steppes.

Once we had put enough distance between us and the bulk of the army, we veered off the Roman road and made camp in a fallow field. We ate cold rations, swallowed it down with wine, and retired to the furs.

The following morning we rode north, heading for the Astico Valley in the foothills of the Alps. Just before midday, we trotted across a bridge of stone and wood spanning the river and headed north and west up the broad valley. As we progressed deeper into the passes, the towering mountains closed in and we arrived at a small Roman settlement.

We reined in a hundred paces from the cluster of houses, dismounted, and walked our horses closer in an attempt not to alarm the townsfolk.

I noticed a greybeard harvesting early grapes from a vineyard enclosed by a low stone wall.

"Greetings", I said, and inclined my head.

"Well met, soldier", the old farmer replied, shielding his eyes with an open palm. He studied my uniform, which was clearly Roman. "Are you on the emperor's business, son?"

"I am", I replied, and gestured at the towering peaks to the west. "I require the services of a man who is familiar with the mountain tracks. Do you know of a goatherd that will be willing to guide us in exchange for coin?"

The man issued a chuckle, and with a sweeping gesture indicated the luscious green fields that surrounded us. "There are more than enough pastures in the valley to feed our animals", he said. "Why would we want to send our goats into the domain of the wolves and the bears? One would have to be mad to venture into the wilderness."

I noticed Hostilius suppress a snicker and heard him mumble. "I told you so, didn't I."

Before I could reply to the farmer, his own words must have jogged his memory and he gestured to the tombstones on the other side of the road. "Maybe there is someone who can help you."

I noticed movement in the graveyard. A young man in his early twenties was reclining in the afternoon sun with his back against a stone.

"No one knows what is wrong with Secundus", the farmer mused as he waved and smiled at the dullard, who returned the gesture. "Some say that the gods are punishing him, others that his humors are out of balance." He pulled up his shoulders in a shrug. "But what is sure is that something is not right behind that boy's eyes."

"His parents are rich folk from Patavium whose coin bought him a *domus* in town", the man said, and pointed at a cluster of houses farther down the road. "But poor Secundus spends most of his time in the mountains doing the gods know whatever it is that madmen do. He's the only one who knows those hills over yonder."

"I've done extensive reading about mental disorders", Diocles revealed with pride. "The Stoics have interesting theories on how to assist and communicate with people suffering from these ailments."

"Then show us how your scrolls work in practice", Hostilius suggested.

Diocles rose to the Primus Pilus's challenge and walked off to engage the man who was still leaning with his back against a stone. I heard my aide exchange greetings before he sat down beside the simpleton, followed by a lengthy muted conversation.

Hostilius, who possessed a suspicious nature, had a few enquiries of his own which he directed at the farmer. "This Secundus doesn't have a starved look about him", he said. "Who feeds him?"

"Once a month a cartload of food arrives from Patavium", the farmer said. "All kinds of expensive stuff - joints of smoked meat, baskets of dates and even amphorae of wine. Told you his folks are rich."

"For how long does he vanish into the mountains?" Hostilius asked.

"About a week at a time", the farmer replied.

"Hmm", Hostilius mused, thinking on the old man's words.

Diocles came to his feet and stomped towards us, a scowl of defeat plastered on his face. The Primus Pilus gestured that we should meet him halfway.

"He's a pleasant enough fellow", my aide said. "But he is not willing to help us. The advice of the Stoics is worthless."

I expected Hostilius to gloat, yet the opposite happened. "Don't be too hard on yourself, Greek", the Primus Pilus said, and indicated the dullard. "Secundus is no madman . I'll bet my last *sestercius* that he's a smuggler."

A frown creased Diocles brow.

"Every week a cart arrives from Patavium", Hostilius said. "And we all know the city's known for its expensive wool cloaks and unaffordable wine."

"Both items attract a high rate of customs duty when it crosses the borders of the provinces", Diocles mused. "And he poses as a madman to hide his dealings."

"I'll be right back", Hostilius said, "after I've had a word with our friend."

Chapter 8 – Mountains

Before nightfall we made camp outside the settlement. We saw little of the townsfolk, who kept their children inside and their doors bolted.

Although I discreetly posted guards around our guide's *domus*, he did not attempt to abscond during the hours of darkness.

The following morning, we broke our fast on millet porridge and struck camp before the sun appeared from behind the eastern peaks.

Our guide rode beside Diocles and me, leading the way along a rough dirt track that meandered up into the hills.

Secundus was the son of a wealthy merchant from Patavium. Being the youngest of seven children, he stood no chance to inherit the business. When he became a man, his father handed him a fat purse and told him to make his own way. As is often the case with gifted gold, the coin was squandered on all sorts of debauchery. With Patavium being a bastion of moral standards, he soon ended up falling foul of the city authorities, which was an embarrassment to his family.

Secundus's father manufactured fine-woven, fur-lined cloaks that were highly sought after, especially by the nobility in

Gaul. The exorbitant prices attracted equally exorbitant taxes. Not wishing to join the legions, he had come up with the scheme of smuggling a portion of his father's wares past the imperial tax collectors - which turned out to be a lucrative arrangement. To ensure that his forays into the passes did not raise too many questions, the young man had played the part of an idiot. In return for his services, we agreed to look the other way. It was a small price to pay to save Italia from the depredations of the Alemanni.

Our guide had been traversing the passes for close on three years. For all his faults, he knew the mountains like the back of his hand. Secundus was not only not a madman, but he was educated and blessed with a keen mind. Late morning, we were watering our horses when he approached me. "Legate", he said, and gestured at the warband of Carpiani congregating on the banks of the river. "I assume that you will be ambushing the Germani who are moving down the Via Claudia Augusta?"

I must have nodded.

"Even a dullard can see that your *foederati* warriors are excellent horsemen", he said, grinning at his own jest. "But if the Germani follow you back into the mountains, it will be better to be on foot, I think."

"How do you know?" Hostilius asked.

Our guide lowered his gaze in shame. "Let's just say that more than once men on horseback have tried to, er… apprehend me on these tracks", he replied. "And they failed."

I deferred to Gordas, who thought on Secundus's words while chewing on a sliver of dried goat meat. "The boy may be right", the Hun conceded reluctantly. "If the tracks are as bad as he says, and we are pursued, it will be better to be on foot."

"How far are we from the Roman road where we will ambush the Alemanni?" Hostilius asked.

"We will be there by tomorrow afternoon", Secundus replied. "But we still have to get across Dis Pater's Pass." He gestured to the green banks of the river. "This is the last place with enough room to leave the horses. Tonight we will have to sleep on the track."

Heeding the advice of our guide, we decided to leave most of our mounts behind. Apart from Gordas, of course, who insisted that his Hun mare was every bit as surefooted as a Carpiani. Every ten men were assigned a packhorse to carry furs and quivers. Similarly, Gordas, as a quid pro quo for retaining his mount, agreed to strap our baggage to his saddle.

With the prospect of loot waiting on the other side of the passes, it proved difficult to find volunteers willing to stay behind to look after the horses. Eventually I was forced to offer each man who remained two gold aurei as payment. The coin persuaded a dozen men, mostly older warriors who dreaded the journey, or those who had enough experience to know that a bird in the hand is better than two in the bush.

* * *

"Why is it called Dis Pater's Pass?" Hostilius asked as we walked along the track, which was far less steep that I had anticipated.

"I don't think it is the official name", Secundus replied. "But I would like to believe that if the dark god designed a pass, it would be like the one ahead of us."

"It's because you haven't marched with the legions, smuggler", Hostilius scoffed, and gestured at the Carpiani trudging behind us. "For tribesmen it will be challenging, but if you've served under the standard it's just another stroll in the Roman Forum."

The cool, fresh mountain air was pleasant compared to the stifling heat and the suffocating dust of the Po Valley in summer. We were shielded from the harsh mid-summer sun by tall oaks, chestnuts and elm trees that flourished on the banks of the cobbling river bordering the path. Unencumbered by weapons and food rations, our march along the meandering track felt more like a stroll in Hostilius's proverbial forum than a slug through the mountains. We spoke of old times, chewed on dried meat, and sucked on our wineskins.

As the slope gradually became steeper, the deciduous trees made way for giant spruces and sweet-smelling pines and the conversation waned. Unused to marching, I wiped the perspiration from my forehead and noticed that there were pearls of sweat on the Primus Pilus's brow. Diocles and our guide were both breathing hard. Only Gordas seemed unperturbed, relaxed in the saddle of his scraggy mount with a smug smile on his scarred face.

It did not last long.

Soon a frown of concentration furrowed the Hun's brow as his mare struggled to keep its footing on the scree-covered path that a long-gone people had carved into the side of the cliff. Even though I was on foot, from time to time I was forced to grab hold of a protruding rock or root to make sure that I did not embarrass myself in front of my friends.

We rounded the next bend in the track and the sight made Gordas swing down from the saddle. A recent storm must have triggered a landslide, covering the already dangerous slope with a layer of boulders, mud and uprooted trees. At the top of the incline a rickety arrangement of lashed-together logs spanned a deep gorge. A few feet above the structure, which I do not wish to refer to as a bridge, a dark, foreboding hole loomed in the mountain.

"Dis Pater's Pass is an apt name", Hostilius mused as he paused to catch his breath. "Although I would have named it 'Dis Pater's arse'."

It took the largest part of the remaining daylight hours to haul the horses up the slope and across the logs. Were it not for the fact that our packhorses were of Scythian stock, we would not have had any other option but to leave them behind.

* * *

"If my calculations are accurate the invaders will pass the place of ambush the day after tomorrow", Diocles said while he filled his cup from an amphora.

"That means that we have to be on the other side of the passes by tomorrow evening", Hostilius said, and fixed our guide with a stare.

"We are about ten miles from the Via Claudia Augusta", Secundus said, pointing west.

"Distance means nothing in these hills", Hostilius said. "We travelled less than a mile the whole afternoon."

"Tomorrow will be easier, tribune", our guide promised.

"It better be", the Primus Pilus replied. "For the sake of Italia and for yours, smuggler."

Chapter 9 – Via Claudia Augusta

Although the winding track that followed the south-facing slope of the ravine was without a doubt less challenging than Dis Pater's Pass, it was far from easy to navigate. But we were determined to reach the Via Claudia Augusta before dark, and even more importantly, before the enemy column arrived.

The road remained reasonably flat until late morning when the already steep slopes of the valley morphed into sheer cliffs. The farmers and hunters of old who had created the track possessed not the manpower nor the skills to cut into solid rock, which meant that the path disappeared altogether.

Secundus pointed to the river fifteen feet below. "From here on, that's the road", he said, and led us down the cliffside to the valley floor.

We picked our way along the mostly dry and sandy riverbed until we arrived at a junction where the stream spilled into a larger river. At that moment, a lone traveller appeared from around a bend in the ravine. My hand instinctively dropped to the hilt of my sword, but before I bared my blade I recognised the man for what he was.

He wore a long-sleeved, undyed woollen tunic that extended down to his ankles. In his right hand he carried the staff of a shepherd. Around his neck he wore a wooden cross suspended from a leather thong. His body was thin, almost emaciated, his hair lank and cheeks unshaven, but his dark eyes shone with religious fervour.

"*Maranatha*", the man said, and raised his right hand in a blessing.

"Greetings, holy man", I reciprocated.

Just then a group of about thirty men, women and children trudged from around the same bend. They appeared dishevelled and fearful, with more than one nursing some wound or other.

"The serpent is slithering down from the mountains", the monk said, indicating the way they had come. "The followers of the Evil One is devouring all in their path. Have a care, stranger, tomorrow the barbarians will swarm these lands."

It was clear that the man was a follower of Christ leading his flock to safety.

"Where are you taking these people, priest?" Hostilius asked.

The holy man used his staff to indicate the far wall of the canyon, a rockface that rose high into the sky. "I live alone in the caves, devoted to the Lord", the monk said. "But I cannot stand idly by while my fellow believers are slaughtered."

"The Alemanni will find you and your followers", Hostilius warned.

"No", the man replied with a confidence that was hard to comprehend, and banged the butt of his staff upon the ground. "The Lord will not allow the spawn of the Devil to pass beyond this point."

Mayhap it was the words of the priest, but I believe that Arash, or maybe even the monk's God, whispered into my ear as I studied the surrounding cliffs.

"May your God protect you", I said, and indicated for the monk to resume his journey.

He nodded and went on his way.

I used my chin to gesture to the slopes behind us. "Gordas, take three hundred of the Carpiani, go back the way we came and make your way onto the ledges. Make sure each of your bowmen has two full quivers strapped to his belt."

* * *

With the sun at its zenith, Hostilius, Diocles and I led the remaining seven hundred archers into the valley of the Athesis. As we descended the ravine we laid eyes on the Via Claudia Augusta, the broad road that connected Italia with the provinces north of the Alps. Beyond the Roman road lay fields, pastures, orchards and vineyards that abutted the banks of the river.

The slope to the east of the roadway was covered in ancient forests of maple, chestnut, birch and oak, right up to the cobbles. In the heyday of the Empire, when the men of the tribes did not dare to rouse the ire of the Romans, peace reigned, and the legions ensured that the sides of the roads were clear of growth. Those days were long gone.

A century of neglect had seen the trees and undergrowth encroach on the paved surface, which enabled us to approach without fear of being seen by travellers using the road.

Not that there were any travellers.

Apart from a small band of about a dozen horsemen advancing from the north, the road and fields bordering the riverbank were deserted.

Hostilius, Diocles and I crouched five paces from the cobbles, screened by a thicket of bilberry bushes flourishing at the base of a chestnut tree. We remained motionless and silent. Soon the animals that had been disturbed by our passage were going about their usual business.

A muscular warrior on a brown gelding led the riders. Silver and gold torques were clasped around his oaken arms.

He raised a palm, causing the band to rein in a few paces from our hiding place. Despite the heat of summer, the skin of a brown bear was draped around his otherwise naked torso. I assumed that the use of the cloak was for aesthetic purposes because it had the effect of making his broad, muscular shoulders appear even bulkier. The leader snorted to gather phlegm into his throat before expelling the gob onto the cobbles. He reached for an aleskin that hung from his saddle, sucked on the bone spout for long, belched, and wiped the foam from his plaited beard with the back of his free hand.

A ratty man riding abreast of the leader extended his hand and accepted the skin with a nod while his beady eyes scanned the undergrowth for anything untoward.

"You are wasting your time and mine, Faramund", the big man growled in their native tongue, while the ratty one's eyes darted from tree to tree. "The Romans have bribed Scythian sheep herders to attack us. Unlike us, the sheep lovers are too cowardly to face their enemy beard to beard with a blade in the fist." He gestured at the surrounding mountains. "Our scouts swear that no army of horsemen can navigate these defiles."

Faramund sniffed the air like a feral beast, then, at long last, he seemed to relent and he lay back in his saddle. "My job is to find our enemies, Stithulf", he said, "and your job is to kill them when I do."

"Our scouts have already spotted Roman mercenary horsemen. They will come from the north while the rest of their meagre force wait for us at the southern end of this valley. They think they can trap us between their two armies." He slammed his balled fist onto an open palm for effect. "They believe that they will be able to crush us between the hammer and the anvil."

Faramund seemed slightly concerned by the big man's performance.

Stithulf leaned over and slapped the ratty one on the back. "We have nothing to fear from horsemen in this valley", he said. "On open, flat ground, Scythian horsemen are formidable, but in the confines of this pass they will be useless against our spears."

At that moment, a group of half a dozen riders appeared in the distance, galloping in from the south.

Before long, they arrived.

"Lord Stithulf", one said, and inclined his head. "It is as you said. The black riders of the Romans have closed off the southern end of the valley."

"How many?" Stithulf asked.

"Not more than five thousand", the scout replied.

A feral sneer split Stithulf's bearded lips and his arm came around in a sweeping gesture. "We will wipe the Romans aside like a wolfpack scatters mice", he stated with confidence.

"We will string up their corpses just like we did to those Romans in the town", Faramund said, clearly excited at the prospect.

Hostilius stiffened at the ratty one's words, the muscles in the Primus Pilus's jaw clenching and unclenching. I recognised the warning signs and took his shoulder in a grip of iron to prevent him from doing something he would later regret.

"You are getting ahead of yourself, Faramund", Stithulf said. "Let us ride to tell Lady Braduhenna what we have learned."

By the way he said her name, it was clear that the witch was more to him than just a war matron.

Stithulf jerked his horse's head around and led the group of Alemanni north at a canter.

Chapter 10 – Black

The Alemanni scout slowly crouched his way through the underbrush. Every couple of paces he came to a complete halt and purposefully moved his head from side to side. Like all experienced huntsmen he employed not only his eyes, but also his ears and nose.

Sensing danger, the man suddenly stopped dead in his tracks, his hand dropping to the hilt of his weapon.

Without a sound I came to my feet, less than a pace behind the Germani. I reached out, clamped my open palm around the scout's mouth, and rammed the blade of my dagger into his neck just below the base of his skull, severing his spine. He went limp in my arms and I allowed the corpse to slide from the iron before gently laying it down on the carpet of leaves.

Hostilius rose from the shrubbery, ten paces distant. At his feet was the body of another scout, the head twisted at a grotesque angle. "That's the last of the vermin", he whispered.

I pressed my hand to my mouth and imitated the warbling of a yellow-billed chough. The forest seemed to come alive as seven hundred Carpiani rose from their hiding places and advanced to the edge of the trees. The Scythians were spread out in a long line, two paces separating the bowmen.

Concealed by the mogshade, I kneeled, bent the limbs of my horn bow with the aid of my legs, and slipped the loop of a sinew string onto the horn nock. Even as I took four arrows into my draw hand, my eyes never left the column that was creeping south along the Roman road.

The baggage train of the foe was spread out along three, maybe four miles. Although the army of Goths that Tharuarus had brought to Roman Macedonia months before dwarfed the army of the Alemanni, sixty thousand men were still a force to be reckoned with. In fact, it was one of the largest barbarian armies that had ever invaded Italia.

Less than twenty paces away, slaves clutching leather thongs led teams of bellowing oxen. The tired beasts strained against their yokes to pull the wagons creaking under the weight of Roman loot. Groups of warriors were randomly dispersed among the carts. Some strode along at a leisurely pace, while others hitched a ride, their legs dangling over the sides, all the while jesting and laughing raucously.

Five paces to my left, the Carpiani commander put an arrow to his string. He met my gaze and issued a nod to indicate that he and his men were ready.

I looked up and noticed that the sun was already low in the sky. Moments later, I heard faraway cries of alarm, followed by the wails of Goth war horns.

"That must be Hlodwig giving the Alemanni stragglers a taste of Gothic iron", Hostilius whispered from behind me where he impatiently leaned on the boar spear he had brought along for close-quarters work.

Knowing that the Goths were engaged with the rearguard of the enemy, I pulled the string to my ear, exhaled, and released. The arrow flew true and slammed into the temple of a ruddy-bearded warrior lounging on top of a canvas-covered load. He toppled sideways, the leg of the corpse catching in a wheel. Three spokes sheared off before the wagon ground to a shuddering halt.

Before my second shaft claimed another of the foe, seven hundred Scythian arrows thudded into Germani flesh. Although many enemy warriors fell, some managed to escape the rain of metal. The wail of a ramshorn echoed from amongst the wagons as the survivors signalled to their brethren that the baggage train was under attack. But the column of the invaders stretched for miles along the Roman road, and I knew that it would take at least five hundred heartbeats for them to respond in force.

Having nothing better to do than to watch, Hostilius issued a comment. "I thought we weren't supposed to damage the wagons?" he said, and pointed to where the mangled corpse had broken a wheel.

"It was an accident", I replied, and released another arrow.

The aim when attacking a baggage train is to destroy as much supplies as possible, and, in addition, to incapacitate the wagons either with fire, taking axes to the wheels, or slitting the throats of the draught animals. It would leave the foe short of supplies and with few other choices than to head home with their remaining loot.

It was not what I wanted to achieve. I wished to make an example of the Alemanni, and in order to do so, they needed to continue their advance. My intention was to whittle down their numbers, shatter their confidence and make them look over their shoulders.

Having injured or killed hundreds of warriors in the first assault, the Carpiani bowmen advanced. Many Germani were hiding behind or underneath wagons in the hope that the attackers would be distracted in the confusion of taking loot, but they were in for a surprise.

I had threatened the Carpiani with certain death if they as much as touched the wagons, and I felt confident that my reputation as a man devoid of mercy would stay their hands.

The Scythians moved amongst the wagons in groups of three, riddling the survivors with their arrows. Hostilius and Diocles joined me. Our scout, Secundus, refused to remain in the forest by himself so he reluctantly trailed behind.

"Would you look at that!" Diocles exclaimed. He pointed at three wagons that were surrounded by corpses of well-appointed warriors, indicating that the cargo was of importance. The carts carried a collection of cages housing goats, sheep, geese and chickens. A large bull was tied to the rear of the wagon.

"By the gods", Hostilius said, his hand searching for his amulet.

Caged animals on the back of a wagon is not an unusual sight, but these ones had one striking thing in common. It was a well-known fact that the dark deities of the underworld could only be appeased by the sacrifice of black animals, which were extremely difficult to come by. It seemed that the Alemanni had amassed a good stock of them to allow Braduhenna to invoke the power of the tribe's gods.

"This must be the witch's wagon", the Primus Pilus said, concern written all over his face. "For the sake of the gods, don't kill the animals, Domitius. If you do, the dark gods will hound our shades for all eternity."

"The gods of Rome have given us an opportunity", I said, and opened the door of a cage. At least forty black chickens scuttered to freedom and disappeared into the undergrowth bordering the road. "When Braduhenna has nothing to sacrifice to her dark gods, her warriors will interpret it as a bad omen."

"Better hurry up", Hostilius said, pointing to where the Carpiani were releasing arrows at the reinforcements making their way towards us.

"Chase the bull into the river", I told Diocles, while dozens of black sheep and goats darted past us into the woods.

Hostilius had just unlashed the door of the last cage when, somewhere to the rear, a cacophony of screams split the air. I swung around, ready to release a shaft at a charging foe, but the scene playing out almost made me drop the arrow.

A bearded warrior brandishing a spear had slipped from underneath a tarpaulin where he had been hiding, intent on skewering the nearest attacker, who turned out to be Secundus.

The brute would have been successful, but a Germani girl, who wore the dress of a slave, vaulted onto his back before I could put an arrow in him. She screamed like a fishwife, repeatedly stabbing her victim with a dagger. The chainmail protecting the Alemanni's torso must have been Roman because it kept the blade at bay. The warrior desperately tried to dislodge the girl, but she clung to him like a famished tick.

Two paces from the pair, Secundus stood frozen. His back was pressed against the wheel of a wagon, an expression of horror plastered on his clean-shaven face.

The girl must have realised the futility of her actions and instead reached around the warrior's neck to try and open his throat.

Her attempt proved only partially successful.

The man discarded his spear to clutch at his bleeding neck, but managed to get a hand on the girl's arm. He plucked her from his back, threw her to the ground as if she were a rag, and slid his dagger from the sheath.

At that moment our guide found his courage, or mayhap the gods intervened. Secundus grabbed the discarded spear from the cobbles, issued a roar that would have made a lion proud, and drove the iron tip into the brute's neck before he could finish the girl off.

Another foe came rushing towards Secundus, intent on avenging his fallen comrade. Our guide bravely stepped into the warrior's path to protect the girl, but Hostilius was ready. The Primus Pilus skipped forward and, using his spear haft as a club, struck the barbarian a massive blow to the side of his helmeted head. The man dropped to his knees, swayed, and fell facedown onto the cobbles.

"Who are you?" Hostilius asked the girl in her native tongue.

"I am Ganna of the Semnones", she said, and struggled to her feet, bleeding from a wound to the leg.

The Primus Pilus used his chin to gesture to the forest. "Go", he said, and indicated the horde advancing from up the road. "Before the Alemanni get here or I change my mind."

She stood rooted to the spot, her jaw set in defiance. Secundus found another tranche of courage and stepped in between the bull-like Primus Pilus and the girl. "She saved my life, tribune. Either she comes with us, or I stay."

If there was one thing Hostilius respected more than anything, it was bravery. The Primus Pilus's sneer slowly morphed into a grin. He grounded his boar spear and slapped Secundus's shoulder. "You should have joined the legions, boy", he said. "But have a care. Semnones women are feral creatures."

"How do you know that?" our guide asked.

"Because I'm married to a Goth", Hostilius replied, and skipped forward to drive his spear into another crazed savage intent on killing us.

"Come", I said, and pointed to where the Scythian bowmen were slowly backpedalling towards us, hardly holding the advancing horde at bay with their arrows. "We have to retreat before the Alemanni reach us."

Ganna tried to walk with Secundus's assistance, but the wound to her leg caused her to stumble and fall.

Hostilius issued a sigh, bent over at the waist, picked up the lithe girl as if she weighed naught, and draped her over his shoulders. "I'm only carrying her as far as the hills", he said, and gestured to our guide to lead the way into the trees.

If the Primus Pilus possessed the gift of glimpsing the future, he would probably have volunteered to carry her all the way to Verona.

Chapter 11 – Dragon

Thousands of barbarians surged into the woods bordering the road. Judging by the confident way Secundus weaved along the web of game paths, I was sure that fleeing from the authorities was an integral part of his trade.

Like most Germani, the Alemanni were skilled woodsmen and they had no trouble remaining on the trail of such a large host. Whenever the path straightened out, a dozen or so Carpiani lingered and sent an indiscriminate volley of shafts in the direction of the onrushing warriors. The tactics managed to slow our pursuers down for a span of heartbeats until the frenzy of the chase once again made them throw caution to the wind.

Fortuna favoured us. By the time the woods thinned and the paths spilled into the canyon that led to the mountains, our pursuers were yet to get within spear distance of the slowest of the Scythian bowmen. Hostilius was blowing hard, his face red with exertion.

We struggled on across the dry riverbed, trudging through the soft sand that gave way beneath our feet. Hostilius came to a halt, and many of our bowmen jogged past.

"Let me carry her", I said, and reached to take the girl from my friend.

The look in the Primus Pilus's eyes suggested that he wished to spurn my offer, but instead he issued a nod. I relieved him of his burden and we plodded on, moving only slightly faster than marching pace.

We had not gone fifty paces when the Semnones girl, who was facing the rear, issued a shout of warning. "Leave me", she said. "They are going to catch us. I am too heavy."

I stole a glance over my shoulder and spied a mob of barbarian warriors racing towards us along the riverbed. Three hundred and fifty paces in front of us loomed the dark cliffs of the junction where we had earlier left Gordas in charge of the three hundred Carpiani.

"We might still make it", Diocles said from beside me as the last of the Scythians drew level with us.

The familiar twang of hemp and sinew bowstrings reached my ears. In the distance, hundreds of arrows left the cliff face and rose to the heavens.

Most experienced bowmen can predict with great accuracy where an arrow will fall. I knew that we were in trouble.

"Come!" I shouted, and scraped together the last remaining strength in my sinews to sprint and avoid the rain of death.

Behind me I heard the shouts of the pursuers readying to cast their spears. I could go no further. My legs collapsed from under me and I went sprawling onto the sand. But a fist of iron gripped the back of my armour and yanked me to my feet. "Let's get going, Domitius", Hostilius grunted. "You can lie down and rest after we've killed the bastards."

I had hardly gained my feet when the first volley of arrows slammed into the lead ranks of the Germani, creating the impression that they had run into an invisible wall. Dozens of foes fell to the ground, writhing in pain, futilely clutching at feathered shafts. I was still gawking at the sight when the second volley claimed an equally bloody harvest.

The Alemanni were brave, but fools they were not. The advancing ranks crouched down and took the third volley on the wood of their shields.

Secundus and Diocles led the way up the steep cliffside path, the slave girl supported between them.

Although the tribesmen had come to a halt just beyond the range of the Carpiani arrows, the canyon below was slowly filling with barbarians.

Gordas stared down at the writhing mass of fur-clad clansmen who were working themselves into a frenzy. "They have more warriors than we have arrows", the Hun stated flatly.

"The sun will be gone soon", Hostilius said while waving his hand in a dismissive gesture at the overcast sky. "You know how these savages are - as soon as it gets dark, all they're interested in is to sit next to their fires and drink themselves senseless. Besides, there's no moon tonight and how in hades are they going to negotiate the path if they can't even see their filthy hands in front of their faces?"

The Primus Pilus sucked the last drops from his wineskin. "It won't be long before they get thirsty and then we can all head home."

"We should remain vigilant", I cautioned. "In case their appetite for slaughter becomes greater than their thirst for ale. If they catch us on the path they will kill us to a man."

I had hardly uttered the words when the far walls of the canyon were illuminated by an eerie glow that became increasingly brighter. Eventually, a long line of warriors arrived from the direction of the main enemy column and started to distribute the flaming brands they carried.

As darkness seeped in from the east, more brands were lit until it appeared as if a river of fire flowed along the valley floor. Soon the chants and war songs of the mob snuffed out the will of individuals. The horde started to move as one, morphing into a living thing - a mythical fire-breathing serpent.

Then the creature went silent, as if drawing breath, and from its maw it spewed flames. Hundreds of torch-bearing savages charged across the open ground to reach the path that ascended the cliff.

I drew the bowstring to my ear, exhaled, and sent a shaft into their ranks. Before my arrow struck, another followed in its wake.

We sent volley after volley into the body of the firedrake, but it seemed to help naught. We wounded, maimed and killed hundreds, mayhap thousands, but still the foe kept coming. I sent a broad-bladed arrow into the leg of a warrior who had succeeded in reaching the bottom of the cliff path, but when I reached into my quiver to strike down another, no shafts remained. Gordas's men had not taken part in the ambush of the baggage train, so they were the only ones with arrows remaining in their quivers.

"My people believe that only magic can defeat the *wyrm* of fire", I heard Ganna whisper from where she clutched Secundus's arm.

I knew that we could not hold back the onslaught for long, so I prayed to Arash to show me a way to defeat the dragon.

I opened my eyes.

On the opposing cliff-face I noticed human shapes backdropped against the dim light of fires that burned inside what I presumed was a system of caves.

Hostilius must have noticed. "Don't pay those fools any heed", he said, and drew his *gladius*. "It must be the priest and his followers we came across yesterday. The only thing that will save our hides is iron, not a holy man tending to his flock."

The storm of arrows soon dwindled to a trickle, allowing the attackers to gain a foothold on the steep track.

I drew my sword and gripped my dagger in my left fist. Gordas, Diocles, Hostilius and I took up position at the top of the narrow path, knowing that only two or three could bring themselves to bear at the same time. Behind us, the Carpiani were drawing their blades, very aware of the fact that the four of us would only be able to hold back the wave of warriors for a short time.

We had no shields, but neither did the Germani who needed their hands free to wield torches.

A blonde warrior sporting a topknot and a braided beard powered up the path, a war axe in one fist and a flaming brand in the other. The man wore an old-style mail byrnie that extended to the waist and was kept in place by a broad leather belt. His knee-length leather *braccae* were undyed and matched his crude boots. He drew the axe back over his right shoulder, a spray of spittle accompanying his war cry.

The axe is a devasting weapon in the hand of a skilled man, but the warrior I faced was probably a woodsman rather than a master who would have known that a longsword's reach exceeded that of an axe's. He chopped down at my waist as if he was about to fell a tree.

But trees do not fight back, and neither do trees wield blades.

I lunged forward and the tip of my sword entered his neck. The Germani was caught halfway in the swing and the momentum of his axe, clutched in a death grip, pulled the corpse from the path and it tumbled into the abyss.

Gordas's battle-axe whirred past my head, the spike striking another helmetless brute in the forehead. The man on his heels wore armour of good quality. I blocked the downward strike of his blade, but before I could turn defence into attack, Hostilius used the extended reach of his boar spear and lunged, opening the large artery in the warrior's lower leg. He issued a screech of pain and toppled backwards, taking at least three of his comrades with him.

We killed a dozen men, maybe two, but then I felt Hostilius's hand on my armour as he pulled me to the rear to allow rested men to replace us.

While I tried to catch my breath, I looked down at the sea of torches and heard the screams of Carpiani as the foe sent experienced fighters up the path. Enemy warriors still poured into the canyon, their numbers seemingly undiminished by the men we slew.

"It doesn't look good, does it?" Hostilius said. Judging by Diocles and Gordas's expressions, they agreed with my friend's assertion.

Again, I noticed movement on the opposing cliff. In the dim light of the torches, I saw the Christian priest standing on a ledge, sixty feet above the heads of the Germani horde. His open palms were extended above his head while he chanted what I believed to be a prayer to his God. Ten paces farther along the overhang, his followers were toiling in the dark.

Hostilius passed me his wineskin, but before I could take a swig, I heard an unearthly sound coming from across the rift. Not only did I hear it, but I felt a grating shudder through the soles of my feet, which resonated in my bones. It was as if one of the titans in Diocles's scrolls were slowly tearing off a piece of the mountain with his bare hands.

"Saturn's scythe", Hostilius swore, causing me to turn my head away from the ravine. "What in hades…"

The Primus Pilus got no further and his lower jaw dropped in surprise.

I swung my head back round.

A boulder as large as two ox wagons was slowly toppling from the cliff face opposite us. I was spellbound as the massive chunk of rock tore free from its age-old bonds, fell over the edge, and struck a protruding ledge with a bone-jarring shudder. The impact did not slow down the stone, but propelled it forward, launching it right into the horde below.

In horrified fascination we watched as the boulder decimated the enemy ranks. The massive rock careened along the canyon floor, crushing all in its path. When eventually the stone thudded to a halt, the war cries of the foe were replaced by the wails and moans of hundreds of injured warriors.

From where the rock once stood, twenty men with wooden poles stared at us, their eyes wide at what they had managed to accomplish.

The Christian priest, his prayer finished, lowered his arms and turned back to the caves.

Chapter 12 – Lever

The boulder had crushed not only the bodies of the Alemanni, but also their will to continue the pursuit. Out of respect for the dead, we watched in silence as our demoralised adversaries gathered their fallen and returned whence they came, leaving the valley eerily dark and silent.

Once they had all departed, I sent twenty men down the path to collect as many serviceable torches as possible and, following Hostilius's advice, we braved the mountain track to put as much distance between us and the enemy in case they experienced a change of heart.

A torch-bearing Secundus showed the way. Ganna rode beside him, mounted on a packhorse that our aide led by a rope halter.

"The Christian priest vanquished the fire *wyrm*", Ganna said in passable Latin. "His magic is strong."

"He who strives will find his gods strive for him equally", Diocles quoted from the ancient writings of Euripedes.

"Sounds like Greek nonsense to me", Hostilius stated. "I've heard men say that the gods help those who help themselves, but believe you me, it's a pile of crap."

We all waited for Hostilius to elaborate, but he remained silent. I suspected that it was a deliberate ploy from the Primus Pilus to bait Diocles by exploiting his inquisitive nature.

"Then what might your view be, tribune?" my aide asked, swallowing the hook.

"The gods help those whom they favour", the Primus Pilus replied with a smirk. "It's as simple as that. I've watched men strive to accomplish things by hard work and never attain it, while others, who don't even try, achieve it because they're beloved by the gods."

"So you're saying that hard work is useless", Diocles said.

"Don't put words in my mouth, Greek", Hostilius said. "I'm saying that first and foremost one must strive to attain the gods' favour. Once that is done, work all you want."

By the light of the flickering torch Gordas was carrying, I noticed a deep frown crease my aide's brow.

Hostilius, on the other hand, wore a smirk on his lips. He decided to rub salt into the wound. "If the Christian priest didn't have the favour of their God, his followers would have toiled with their levers all night long without moving that boulder one inch. But because they were favoured, they managed to topple the rock. Not because of their toil."

Diocles cleared his throat to salvage his dignity by continuing the argument. I increased my pace and fell in beside our guide and his newfound love.

"Will you return to the village?" I asked.

"No, legate", he said. "Once I have taken you safely across the passes, I will accompany Ganna on a journey back to her people. I will try to make a living amongst the Semnones."

"Two years ago I was captured by the Alemanni who attacked our clan", Ganna said. "They took me as a slave and sold me to the Romans in Raetia. Three moons ago, a raiding party captured me from the Romans I served. The warrior who took me as a slave was a cruel man. He beat me and I vowed to kill him."

The girl's words explained her actions earlier during the evening.

"Ganna's father is a noble of their tribe", Secundus continued. "She assures me that he will give his blessing on our union."

The two lovers' story seemed much like my own. I, too, had fallen in love with a girl of the tribes and had lived amongst the barbarians for years. "Go where your fate leads you", I said, and slowed my pace, just in time to catch the tail end of Hostilius and Diocles's argument concerning the merit of levers.

* * *

Early morning, two days hence, we said our goodbyes to Secundus and Ganna and led the Carpiani south to join the rest of the Goth cavalry.

"Well, that will be the last time we lay eyes on those two lovebirds", Hostilius said once we were out of earshot. "That boy turned out well for a madman."

We all shared the Primus Pilus's sentiments, but there were bigger things at play. Diocles voiced the concern that gnawed at us all. "The Emperor and the Illyrians will be all that stand between the advancing horde and the riches of Italia", Diocles said. "If the enemy breaks through, the land will burn - maybe even Rome."

"We have slain many of them", Gordas said. "The shades of their dead will whisper words of vengeance into the ears of the living. All the foe has seen from us is men who inflict death before they turn and run. The Alemanni will think that the Romans and their allies are cowards. They will be keen to redden their iron with our blood so that their departed kin can find peace on the other side of the river."

Gordas, being a savage of the worst kind, possessed a deep understanding of the psyche of barbarians. I, too, had the blood of Scythians coursing through my veins.

"And that is the reason why, having sent their brethren on their way across the bridge of stars, the Germani will be baying for the blood of any Roman who dares to stand in their way", I confirmed. "When the Illyrians turn and flee before the spears of the Alemanni, the enemy will pursue them. Especially when they see the emperor amongst our horsemen's ranks."

"We are staking everything on one roll of the dice", Hostilius said. "The Greek is right - Italia will burn if the horde does not pursue the emperor."

Gordas said naught because he was clearly convinced that the barbarians would rather die than forego an opportunity to slake their thirst for revenge.

I, on the other hand, shared Hostilius's concerns. "That is why we have to make sure that the enemy gives chase", I said.

"How can you ever be sure that they will?" Hostilius asked. "Those savages are as unpredictable as wild beasts. They themselves don't even know what they are going to do before they actually do it."

"I disagree", I said. "Braduhenna has spoken an oath before all the gods of Germania that she will not rest until I am dead."

"You're here, not at the Emperor's side", Hostilius said.

"Then we need to remedy the situation", I replied, and turned to face Diocles. "From this moment on, you command the Goth *foederati*", I said. "Do as we have discussed, tribune."

My aide was one of the most intelligent and competent men I had ever come across, so I had no qualms placing the future of Italia in his capable hands.

"I understand, legate, and I will obey", Diocles replied formally, and saluted in the way of the legions.

I reciprocated, indicated for Gordas and Hostilius to follow me, and kicked Kasirga to a gallop.

* * *

Three lone riders are able to move at greater speed than a large body of horsemen, and even more so if those riders are Scythians mounted on the tireless horses of the steppes.

Mid-morning, we galloped into the massive Goth camp on the banks of the Little Medoacus near the town of Vicetia.

While Hostilius and Gordas watered the horses, I sought out Aldara, the commander of the Goths. "Ready your men to ride", I said. "Tribune Diocles commands in my absence. Follow his orders to the letter, no matter what he requires."

Aldara inclined his head. "We know that the god of war speaks through you, lord", he said. "I will obey your ringman's commands because I know they come from the mouth of Teiwaz himself."

* * *

At the grey hour of the wolf, we arrived at the southern end of the Brenner Pass where the Via Claudia Augusta entered the lands of Italia. We were tired and dirty and covered in the dust and grime of the journey.

Marcus, his guards and five thousand Illyrians had made camp next to the Roman road where the meandering river bordered an expanse of flat ground. The pass was narrow at the site, mayhap only half a mile wide. The Germani would not be able to skirt the Illyrians, they would have to vanquish them to taste the spoils of Italia.

While Gordas tended to the horses, Hostilius and I washed the sweat from our tired bodies with the cold water of the Athesis before presenting ourselves to the emperor.

* * *

Once the last of the praetorians had left the tent, I poured wine into four wooden cups - the kind that fighting men use on campaign.

Marcus accepted the vessel with a nod of thanks. "My scouts have already skirmished with the advance riders of the enemy", he said. "Tomorrow, before the sun reaches its zenith, the Germani will arrive at the gates to Italia." The emperor took a small sip and added, "And we will be outnumbered ten to one."

"We must allow them to break through our blockade", I said. "Their infantry will have the advantage in the confines of the pass. We need to lure them onto open, flat ground that suits our cavalry."

Marcus issued a guffaw. "Do not be concerned, Lucius", he said. "Even if we wanted to, it will be impossible to stop the horde from entering Italia."

"Good", I replied.

"You seem confident that they will pursue us", Marcus said. "How can you be sure that the lure of the riches of Italia will not be stronger than their desire to rid the world of the Roman emperor?"

"Braduhenna wants me dead", I explained. "You were there when she made an oath to her god."

Marcus waved his hand in dismissal. "The shade soon forgets old oaths when the eyes are blinded by the glitter of gold."

"True", I replied. "That is why I will remind Braduhenna of her oath."

"Are you planning on sending her a letter or whispering into her ear?" Hostilius asked skeptically.

"Tomorrow when the horde arrives, I will challenge Stithulf, her lover, to single combat", I said.

"Are you sure it is wise?" Hostilius asked, suddenly concerned. "If you kill the witch's man she might lead the horde on a rampage across Italia."

"My plan entails something slightly different", I replied, and shared the details with my friends.

When I was through, Hostilius took a long draught from his cup and reclined with his back against the sofa. "You know, Domitius, you've come up with many daring schemes over the years, but this one might just be the one that gets us all killed."

He leaned forward, slapped his knees with his open palms and stood, a grin suddenly splitting his lips. "That's why I teamed up with you all those years ago - I knew it would never get boring."

Chapter 13 – Parley

I pressed my forefinger onto the *itinerarium*, indicating our position.

"The Via Claudia Augusta approaches Northern Italia along the river valley of the Athesis", I said. "The last few miles before it emerges from the passes, the Roman road is flanked by mountains to the east and west. The range to the west of the road is but a thin strip of peaks that separate the Athesis River Valley from the northern half of a large body of water known as Lake Benacus."

"Yes, yes. We know all that", Hostilius said.

I fixed the Primus Pilus with a glare and received a scowl in reply.

"As I was saying", I continued. "The southeastern side of Lake Benacus is bordered by ground that is mostly flat and therefore ideal for cavalry. As one moves north along the water's edge, the mountains gradually encroach on the lake, creating a funnel of sorts. Eventually, all that remains is a track cut into the slope of the shore."

"If we are fleeing before the barbarians, here is a good place to make a stand", I said, and pressed my finger onto a spot on the map.

"Aren't we going to push ourselves into a corner?" Hostilius said.

"We are", I confirmed. "But the Alemanni will also be trapping themselves without realising it. Diocles will bring his horsemen around from Verona. We will crush them between the Illyrians and the Goth cavalry", I added. "There will be no escape for the invaders."

"It is a good plan", Marcus said, and placed his hand on my shoulder. "But first we need to lure them into your trap."

We were interrupted by the duty tribune stepping into the tent.

"Lord Emperor", he said, and inclined his head. "The enemy is approaching. We await your orders."

"Come", I said. "Let us find out what fate the gods have decided upon."

* * *

The black riders of Rome deployed across the width of the Athesis Valley. Their left flank was anchored against steep granite cliffs and their right protected by the swirling river. The Roman horsemen sat in their saddles unmoving, their lances grounded, waiting for the foe to show himself.

An icy northerly gust came tumbling down the slopes, ruffling the manes of the Illyrians' mounts. It failed to affect the black-clad soldiers who sat like statues hewn from the Black Stone itself. The sudden breeze heralded the approach of a summer storm, and soon dark clouds blotted out the sun as if the gods were setting a sombre stage for the inevitable confrontation.

The first sign of the enemy was a group of riders that rounded a far bend in the road. The dozen or so fur-clad horsemen appeared relaxed, trotting at an easy pace. The Alemanni made no attempt to conceal their approach. The warriors animatedly gestured in our direction, and their shouts of warning that were directed at their brethren behind, echoed off the cliffs.

"I guess they've seen us", Hostilius said drily.

Marcus sat beside me atop a pure white mount. My friend was the perfect embodiment of a warrior king. He sat straight in the saddle, the iron-hard muscles in his forearms twitching as he fiddled with the reins of his stallion. His cuirass, helmet and armour were polished to a brilliant shine. To any fighting man who took a moment to look deeper, it would be clear that it was the armour of a soldier, not the ornate fripperies one would expect from a pampered noble. The pommels of his sword and dagger were worn smooth from a lifetime of training, and stained with the blood of countless enemies of Rome. The purple cloak draped around his shoulders was thick-woven like a soldier's garment - uncomfortable for a hot day, but able to withstand the rigours of a campaign. For the first time in nearly a hundred years the Empire was in capable hands.

Gordas, who possessed the eyesight of an eagle, issued a grunt. "The witch leads the army", he said.

The enemy vanguard had advanced a few hundred paces. Behind them the entire valley was filling up with warriors - thousands upon thousands who outnumbered us more than ten to one.

When six hundred paces separated us from the Alemanni, the wails of war horns echoed off the cliffs and the horde ground to a halt. Judging by the shouts and the scrambling about, it was clear that they were engaged in some toil or other.

"Maybe they want to surrender", Hostilius jested.

Before long, their ranks parted and scores of ox carts were wheeled to the front. The draught animals had been unhitched and in their place, half a dozen warriors were manhandling each carriage.

"A moveable barrier to shield them from a cavalry charge", Hostilius mused. "It's a clever ploy for savages, I'll give them that, but those carts are heavy, even for six men apiece."

"Let's save them the trouble", the emperor said, and nudged his horse forward. Hostilius, Gordas and I fell in behind him.

Earlier I had tried to talk Marcus out of coming to the parley, but my friend would not shy away from putting himself in harm's way. To Hostilius's great satisfaction the emperor had disdained from riding under a branch of truce.

"Maybe we should have opted for a leafy branch", I said when the Alemanni gave no indication of halting their advance.

"We're not here to parley", Hostilius stated. "We're here for blood, and besides, we don't want to appear weak."

I was about to make a case for appearing weak, when the rider heading up the Germani army raised an open palm. In response, shouts reverberated through the milling mass of barbarians, who slowly came to a stop.

We reined in.

Five riders detached from the ranks of the horde and approached at a walk.

I recognised the lead rider as Braduhenna. She was flanked by a greybeard noble as well as two hulking champions. The torques clasped around their bull-like necks and bulging arms showed that they were no strangers to violence. The larger of the two was the warrior, Stithulf, whom I had overheard days before.

We sat unmoving as the other party reined in two horse lengths in front of us.

Braduhenna was no fool, and in her eyes I saw that she recognised Marcus from the day of the ambush near the river.

"Yes", Marcus said in the tongue of the Germani. "Your eyes are not deceiving you. That day by the river, you had the Roman emperor within your grasp, yet you allowed me to slip through your fingers."

My friend's words riled the lady of the Alemanni and an unseemly sneer split her attractive face. "Mistakes are only mistakes if we allow them to happen twice, Roman", she hissed.

Marcus ignored her venom and gestured to the milling thousands that were still filling up the valley. "There is no need for all of you to die", he said. "Turn back, leave your loot behind, and we will allow you to cross the Mother River with your weapons and your lives."

"You and your pleas reek of fear, Roman", Braduhenna spat. "Before the sun sets today, the blood of your warriors will be lapped up by the soil of this land that you have stolen from our ancient allies. Rome is a stain on the land, an abomination of iron and stone that needs to be expunged from history."

She raised her arms above her head like one about to issue a curse. "The prophecy is clear, there will be a great slaughter." As if rehearsed, the horde began to chant, "Death to Rome! Death to Rome! Death to Rome!"

"Maybe you and your rabble will be the ones who get slaughtered", Hostilius blurted out, unable to restrain himself.

Eerily similar sneers of contempt split both Braduhenna and her lover's lips. "We know that you wish to crush us between your Goth slave-soldiers and the black riders", she said. "You are so predictable."

"I will fight *Hard Wolf*", I said, using the champion's Germani name, and my hand went to the hilt of my blade. "So that the lives of your warriors need not be wasted."

Braduhenna failed to suppress a snicker. "Our army will crush your paltry force", she said, and indicated the Illyrians who, I must admit, did appear insignificant when measured against the numbers of the horde. "Besides, there is no benefit for me to agree to it."

"Who reeks of fear now?" Hostilius growled, and spat onto the ground in contempt.

Stithulf nudged his horse forward. "I will fight you, Roman", he said, and slapped his armoured chest with a ham-like fist.

The war matron leered at her lover. "To what end?" she asked.

"So that you may honour your oath to our gods", Stithulf replied. Before Braduhenna could move to stop him, her champion had drawn his longsword.

The Germani believed that once drawn, a blade must be quenched in blood to avoid the wrath of the gods.

"So be it", the witch said. Without another word, she and the oldster abruptly twisted their horses' heads around and galloped back to their lines.

"It is the way of the Germani", I explained. "In a duel, one man may remain to bear the weapons of the champion. For the sake of honour, no others are allowed."

Marcus nodded and he and Gordas returned to the ranks of the Illyrians a hundred paces distant.

Chapter 14 – Retreat

I passed my horse's reins to Hostilius.

"Don't take all day, Domitius", he said, indicating the horde. "Those savages are in dire need of killing, and there are a lot of them."

Ten paces in the direction of the enemy army, Stithulf waited with his sword drawn, winding his blade between high and middle guard. "On second thought, be careful", the Primus Pilus added when he noticed the way the champion handled his weapon. "That one knows his business."

"I hope that you have made peace with the gods you serve, Roman", Stithulf hissed as I approached. "Because you are about to meet them face to face."

I did not reply, but waited for my opponent to make the first move, my blade held in a low guard.

Stithulf knew that I was a man of reputation and he refrained from striking the first blow - a sign of an experienced swordsman.

Hostilius was right - I did not have all day, so I stepped in, aiming an exploratory thrust at my opponent's midriff. He met my blade with his iron and our weapons crossed. Like two bulls locking horns, we gauged each other's strength.

I have heard men boast that strength is not important when wielding a sword, but they are wrong. Great strength allows a warrior's blade to achieve great speed. Speed combined with skill is a deadly combination. But like in war, deception can trump both.

I allowed the big man to push my blade to the side, and a smirk of triumph settled on his bearded face. "You are weak, Roman", he snarled as I retreated.

He followed me in and cut backhanded, his blade sweeping from low to high. I parried, meeting him edge to edge. Our blades locked, and again I allowed him to get the upper hand.

Having twice taken my measure, Stithulf went on the offensive. "Prepare to cross the river", he sneered. His blade flashed high, then low, as he skilfully altered between cuts and thrusts.

The roar of the horde was almost deafening, cheering on their champion who, in their eyes, was close to victory.

Compared to sparring with Cai, whose weapon moved like lighting, Stithulf was merely a child playing at fighting. One after the other I parried his massively powerful strikes until the mob of clansmen, who were urging on their hero to land the killing blow, had worked themselves into a frenzy.

I parried another of the Germani's cuts. By allowing his blade to slide off the flat of my sword, I unbalanced him, causing him to overreach. Before he could prevent it, I had gained the inside line.

"Once go forward, not stop", I heard Cai's words echo in my mind as I advanced, striking blow after blow and never pausing to disengage.

I felt the presence of Arash, and the speed of my strikes became quicker until my blade moved like a silver blur of lightning. Stithulf backpedalled, parrying desperately, the smirk long gone from his scarred face. His foot caught and he sprawled onto the ground, his sword falling from his fist. I stood over him, the razor tip of my blade a hair's breadth from his jugular.

"It… it is not possible", he stuttered in his native tongue. "No man can move that fast."

The cheers of the mob slowly faded. They, like the Illyrians, waited with bated breath for me to strike the killing blow.

I bent down, my blade still pressed against my opponent's throat, and heard a whoosh as Hostilius's boar spear passed over my head, impaling the champion's weapons bearer.

"I said, we haven't got all day", Hostilius scowled, just as I struck Stithulf against the temple with the hilt of my sword.

Hostilius rushed forward and hoisted the prone Germani onto his shoulders, heaved him onto Kasirga's back, and mounted his own gelding. I vaulted into the saddle behind the unconscious warrior before galloping after the Primus Pilus, back to the safety of the Roman ranks.

Our breach of their code of honour momentarily stunned the horde into silence. But their surprise soon turned to anger. An almighty roar of rage erupted from the ranks of the barbarians and they surged forward as one, clambering over the carts that they had wished to use as shields.

* * *

"Signal orderly retreat", Marcus commanded the signifer.

A hundred paces distant, more than fifty thousand screaming barbarian warriors were sprinting towards us, baying for our blood.

"I think your plan is working", Marcus said. On his command, a burly praetorian relieved Kasirga of his burden and lifted Stithulf onto his horse.

Answering the call of the *buccina*, the Illyrians turned their horses' heads away from the onrushing horde. The black riders, as well as their horses, were clad in heavy armour and our opponents knew well enough that, encumbered by iron, we could not outrun them for long.

* * *

It took less than a sixth of a watch to canter to the place where the mountains closed in on the shores of the lake.

While the Illyrians watered their horses, Marcus, Hostilius, Gordas and I ascended the steep hill that protected our rear, or would trap us from escaping the enemy.

A hundred paces up the slope the pines gave way to a granite outcrop, allowing us a commanding view across the open ground to the east. In grim fascination we gaped at the approaching horde. They had widened their front and slowly swept across the landscape like a net dragged by a god.

"I see that it did not take long for the war matron to reassert control over her warriors", Marcus said. "They are not the crazed mob I expected."

Hostilius used a hand to shield his eyes from the sun. "I don't see the Greek and his Goth horsemen", Hostilius remarked.

"Diocles comes", Gordas revealed, pointing in the direction of Verona.

I squinted into the distance and could only just discern a slight haze above the fields.

"How long?" Marcus asked.

Gordas did not reply, his gaze remaining fixed on the horizon for at least a hundred heartbeats. Then his eyes went to the advancing barbarians. "If we fight well, the Greek will be here before they slaughter us all", the Hun remarked, and took a long swig from his wineskin.

* * *

Marcus took an Illyrian helmet from the hand of a praetorian and eased it onto his head. Before accepting a ten-foot-long wooden lance sporting a thin, armour-piercing iron tip, he took a large black oval shield into his left fist and clipped it onto his horned saddle.

"Are you sure about this, Lord Emperor?" I asked, addressing Marcus in the formal way because the ears of his underlings were close.

"Would you sit on your horse at the rear of the ranks if you were emperor, legate?" he said in an equally formal manner.

I grinned in reply before obscuring my own features with a similar chain-hung, blackened helmet sporting a black horse hair plume. Marcus, Hostilius, Gordas and I had ridden into battle countless times and we knew that only a fool placed his destiny in the hands of a stable hand. Meticulously we checked every strap and buckle of our tack and armour before we swung up onto the backs of our horses. Sitting in the saddle, I gripped my shield and made sure that the five lead-weighted war darts were securely strapped onto the inside of the plywood.

I looked to my right where Hostilius was gripping his heavy boar spear and Gordas testing the pull of his horn bow.

Marcus stared at the long line of Germani that were closing in from across the plain. "Let us show them that a cornered beast can be dangerous", he said, and spurred his massive warhorse to a canter.

When a hundred paces separated us from the front rank of the enemy, the bear-cloaked signifer altered the angle of the wolf head standard, causing an unearthly wail to escape from its iron maw. Each Illyrian unclipped a war dart from his shield. At fifty paces the iron wolf screamed again, and five thousand barbed *martiobarbuli* rose high into the cloudy sky.

Thousands of Germani cast their weapons, but their spears found only dirt because the Illyrians had already wheeled about. Few screams of pain emanated from the opposing ranks, as they raised their round shields and the Roman war darts rained down onto the willow wood.

The black riders came around, dressed their line, and kicked their horses to a gallop.

I nodded to the signifer, who issued the command.

Again, we thundered down on their ranks, who had halted their advance in anticipation of our charge. The warriors stood at the ready, their shields raised and their spears hefted.

As one, the Illyrians reined in when fifty paces separated them from the horde.

The stronger amongst the Germani cast their spears at our stationary ranks, but the Roman horsemen contemptuously slapped the handful of missiles from the air with their large oval shields.

"I think you've got them confused, Domitius", Hostilius said from beside me. "They were expecting us to engage."

A charge from the heavily armoured riders would have penetrated deep into the enemy ranks, but even if we had managed to slay ten thousand of them, we would have been surrounded, and the remaining forty thousand would soon have engulfed and overwhelmed us.

My intention was not to slaughter them - not yet, anyway.

Chapter 15 – Shore

For the best part of a third of a watch we played a game of cat and mouse with the Alemanni - we being the mouse, of course. Even though we managed to slow their advance, there was never any doubt that the Germani cat would eventually corner and devour our badly outnumbered force.

Once more, we retreated before the horde. Marcus looked over his shoulder at the shore of the lake that was less than half a mile distant, then he turned his head to glance up at the towering cliffs to the left. "Our horses are almost blown", he said. "The time has come to make a stand."

"They cornered Varus's legions against a wall of timber", Hostilius said from beside me, his voice heavy with determination. "It's payback time. Today we will hem in these savages with a wall of Roman iron and horseflesh."

Years before, through divine inspiration, I had created the Illyrian cavalry, specifically to counter the invasions of the Germani. This new breed of mounted warriors had been inspired by the legendary heavy cavalry of the Roxolani and the feared iron-clad *cataphracts* of the Sasanians.

Nonetheless, there were major differences between the Illyrians and their tribal counterparts. Rather than horses and riders being encased in near-impenetrable armour from head to toe, only the heads, necks, chests and front legs of our warhorses were protected by scale and chain.

Trial and error had seen us discard the heavy, two-handed spear in favour of lighter lances - an innovation that allowed the Illyrians to carry shields. The Roman horsemen relied not only on the crushing impact of a charge to obliterate those who dared to face them, but they also decimated the shield wall of the opposing side with lead-weighted war darts before slamming into their ranks. Whereas the barbarian horses' heavy armour limited them to one, maybe two, all-out charges, the Illyrians' steppe-bred mounts were able to swoop at the enemy multiple times.

But, perhaps because they were Roman, the main distinction was the Illyrians' ability to deploy in orderly ranks as a counter to the barbarian shield wall. Like their legionary counterparts, the Illyrian horsemen were trained to stand shoulder to shoulder to halt the advance of an enemy.

I nodded to Marcus and relayed the orders of the emperor to the signifer.

In response, the Illyrians dressed their line. Advancing at a walk, we slowly closed the gap that separated us from the front rank of the Alemanni. For a span of heartbeats the enemy remained undecided, but then the ramshorns blared and the horde surged forward.

When thirty paces separated us from the enemy, five thousand Roman war darts arced high into the air.

In reply, a swarm of barbarian javelins streaked towards us at a near-flat trajectory.

I twisted slightly to the side, pulling my torso in behind my raised shield. At least two spears were deflected off the sturdy laminated wood, the impacts rocking me in the saddle like blows from a war hammer. Kasirga whinnied in pain as a javelin ricocheted off the thick iron and boiled leather scales encasing his muscular chest.

Just before our *plumbatae* rained down on the enemy, I lowered my lance.

Faced with the impossible choice of raising their shields to repel our descending darts or pulling the willow wood to their chests to beat back our lances, most of the foes chose the latter.

The tall, black-bearded brute charging at me was no exception. Having cast his spear, he drew his longsword. His lips were pulled back in a snarl and white spittle flew from his open maw as he cursed me and my mother in equal parts. I could not fault the way in which he pulled his round shield in tight against his body while his muscular legs powered through the ankle-high grass.

It helped him naught.

My stallion was as taut as a drawn bow, and as my heels touched his sides he lurched forward like an arrow from a string. Aided by the power of my horse, the whetted iron tip of my lance passed straight through the shield and skull of the screaming barbarian to lodge deep in the torso of the warrior behind him. I retained my grip on the haft, and the thin, barbless lance came free as my mount crushed the corpses underneath his hooves. A third warrior, with a war axe drawn back across his shoulder, miscalculated the speed and power of my stallion and collided with his massive iron-encased chest. I heard the crunching sound of bones snapping as the impact spun the his broken body from my field of vision.

The Illyrians were well-trained and reined in before their mounts penetrated too deep into the mass, their three shallow ranks forming a mile-wide wall of horseflesh and iron. In contrast to the Romans, there were no discernible ranks to the horde, although I estimate that the tight-pressed Germani stood fifty paces deep.

Facing unbroken, orderly ranks of cavalry, not dissimilar to a shield wall of the legions, was a novelty for the Germani. At first, warriors heavy with arm rings broke away from the pulsating mob - spear, sword and axe-bearing champions who were eager to prove their courage to their peers. They charged at the Illyrians, confident that the line of horsemen could easily be scattered to the wind.

They died to a man, impaled by ten-foot-long lances that snaked out from the black riders' ranks.

Behind the foe I noticed that the skyline was becoming hazy with dust.

While the milling, chanting mob watched the flower of their warriors perish on the iron of the Romans, their anger reached fever pitch. Howling with rage and bloodlust they surged forward as one.

Less than a mile behind the Alemanni, a lone rider crested the slight rise. He reined in at the top of the incline, taking a moment to assess the battlefield like a thinking man would.

Although the enemy was not yet aware of the threat to their rear, I was not the only one who had noticed Diocles's arrival.

Marcus raised his sword in the air to inspire the Illyrians for one last charge. "Our salvation is at hand, brothers!" he boomed. "We will be the wall against which the invaders will be crushed."

The words of their emperor elicited an almighty cheer from the ranks of the Romans.

The shrill note of a Roman *buccina* emanated from the signifer and echoed across the field to where seventeen thousand Goth riders spilled into view, just behind Diocles.

In quick succession I released my last two darts, gripped my flanged mace in my right fist, a Hun battle-axe in my left, and dug my heels into Kasirga's sides while mouthing a prayer. "Arash, mighty lord of the field of blood, give my mount the strength for one last effort."

With a sound akin to the roar of thunder, the massive warhorses of the Illyrians slammed into the ranks of the invaders.

Caught off-guard by the speed of my horse, the first two warriors facing me failed to bring their weapons to bear. They were crushed by the impact and their corpses trampled to a pulp underneath the hooves. The man trailing behind them hefted his war axe, but collapsed screaming as the six-inch-long blade of a falling *plumbata* pierced his shoulder from above and lodged in a lung. Wheezing, he fell to his knees, his frothy red lips moving in a silent prayer to his gods while he feverishly clutched at the leather fletching, trying in vain to pull out the barbed spike.

A blonde, mailed warrior wearing a sneer of contempt on his lips and a magnificent torque of silver around his upper arm shoved the dying man from his path and lunged at my leg with his spear. I managed to deflect the strike with the blade of my axe, but the tip scored a line along my horse's unprotected ribs. My stallion had been trained for war by the people of the horse and he savagely lashed out in reprisal, clamping his jaws around the mailed shoulder of the foe.

A horse's teeth do not rip flesh like the canines of a wolf, but the unexpected attack distracted the warrior for a heartbeat. He perished as my flanged mace split his riveted helmet and caved in his skull.

I heard a scream coming from my left. From the corner of my eye, I witnessed Hostilius dispatch a Germani with a vicious cut from his spatha. The moment of inattentiveness nearly cost me dearly as a stocky brute rushed in from the opposite side, cutting at my leg with a longsword. Before he could finish his bloody work, a braided rope tightened around his neck and plucked him off his feet, his eyes bulging as he desperately clutched at Gordas's lasso.

The next man to face me brandished his spear in defence while working up courage. The shouts of panic from his comrades caused him to stall his attack and glance over his shoulder. I lunged with my lance, allowing the haft to slide through my fingers until my fist tightened around the bulge of the butt as five inches of iron pierced my opponent's groin.

And then there were none willing to face us. They were suddenly more interested in the happenings behind them, nervously twisting and craning their necks in vain, their view blocked by the mob. The only ones who were able to lay their eyes upon their approaching doom were the weak, old or inexperienced warriors farthest away from the front line.

Like a wave racing over the sea, the Goth horsemen came thundering across the open ground, heading straight for the rear of the Alemanni army.

The time for deception and feigned manoeuvres were long gone. All that remained was to crush those who dared oppose us with brute force. Before the wall of mounted barbarian spearmen had even reached the Alemanni, the men in the rear ranks of the enemy were clambering over their fellows in a desperate attempt to escape what was fast becoming their inexorable fate.

The same Goths who had only weeks before wetted their spear blades with Roman blood now charged into the mass of Germanic invaders.

Unless one has witnessed it for oneself, the sound of thousands of broad-bladed spears almost simultaneously ripping into the unprotected backs of fleeing victims can never be accurately described. But for the ones who will never hear it for themselves, it is best to imagine the sound of biting into an overly-ripe peach, amplified to the volume of roaring thunder.

Spellbound, we watched as the steppe horsemen ploughed through the horde, the more skilful amongst the riders penetrating almost halfway into the mob. The fierce expressions on the bearded faces of the Alemanni were nowhere to be seen. Suddenly we were confronted by the pleading eyes of panicked men who wished to see another sunset.

I was about to ask them to lay down their weapons when the screeches of Braduhenna rose above the screams of the wounded. "If you die like cowards, Teiwaz will banish you from the warrior hall and you will roam the darkness for eternity. Perish with a sword in your fist and tonight you will feast with the brave men of your people."

"Suits me just fine", I heard Hostilius growl from beside me.

He did not wait for the enemy to attack, nor for the command of the *buccina*, but spurred his horse into the horde. "This is for defacing the grave of my *ava*!" he boomed as he brought his blade down, slashing clean through the mailed arm of an Alemanni. "This is for hanging Julius the baker from the tree!" and nearly took off the head of the next warrior in his path.

I realised then that Hostilius, hailing from the small town, had personally known every man whom the Germani had so violently slain and strung up on the branches of the oak outside Cadianum. The Primus Pilus had never spoken about it, but now he gave free rein to the pent-up anger that must have festered inside his mind like a boil ready to burst.

Most of the black riders had suffered at the hands of the invaders in one way or another - be it a comrade killed in battle or mayhap the farm of a father or brother raided and burned. Like a sickness spreading through a town under siege, Hostilius's rage found fertile ground amongst the Illyrians, not excluding Marcus, Gordas and me.

The next moment we were amongst the Germani, venting our anger on the barbarians who had dared to prey on a weakened Empire.

By the time we came face to face with Diocles and his *foederati,* we were covered in the blood of vanquished foes.

My aide greeted us with a nod and slowly turned his head to the right and then left, taking a moment to come to terms with the terrible carnage we had wreaked upon the invaders. "It is safe to say that you have honoured your oath, tribune", he said to Hostilius. "I do not believe there are any left alive."

Chapter 16 – Tax (August 269 AD)

After dark, Hostilius, Gordas, Diocles and I found ourselves outside our quarters. The tents had been pitched on the slope of the mountain underneath ancient pines, four hundred paces upwind of the field of blood. We slaked our thirst on neat wine while fatty cuts of mutton grilled above a blazing wood fire.

"Where's our emperor?" Hostilius asked, and passed me a cup brimming with white wine.

"He is in the *praetorium*, doing what emperors do", I replied while I gazed out over the battlefield that sparkled like the stars in the night sky. Darkness had descended, so the Goth *foederati* moved amongst the dead with torches, stripping the corpses of anything of value, including armour, weapons and even clothing.

"These savages are like vultures, eh?" Hostilius said, and spat out a piece of gristle. "Sometimes I wonder if there is anything they own that hasn't been looted from someone else."

"Rome does it too", Diocles replied, his tone casual. "The only difference is we do it on a grander scale." He used a joint of mutton to indicate the pinpricks of light moving amongst the sea of corpses. "The barbarians relieve the dead of trinkets and coin. Rome relieves the ones it conquers of everything, including their land and their culture. For example, much of the Empire's civilised ways have been stolen from the Greeks."

"And where did the Greeks get it from?" Hostilius asked.

"We invented it, of course", Diocles revealed.

"Of course", Hostilius said, his voice laced with skepticism.

Before Diocles could reply, Gordas tapped Hostilius on the shoulder. "Someone comes", he said.

We heard the crunch of boots on stone, and a man appeared in the circle of light cast by the flames of the cooking fire. He was garbed in the black uniform of the Illyrians.

The decurion saluted in the required manner. "Legate, we have combed the battlefield", he said. "The witch is not amongst the dead."

I did not ask the officer if he was sure of his facts as he was aware of my lack of tolerance for incompetence.

Just then there was another commotion and I dismissed the decurion with a nod.

Marcus approached, surrounded by two *contubernia* of torch-bearing praetorians.

"Leave us", the emperor commanded his men.

"There may still be foes lurking in the darkness, Lord Emperor", the officer of the guard cautioned.

"Who will dare draw a blade in the presence of Legate Domitius and his entourage?" he asked the officer. "Would you?"

The guard's eyes washed over Gordas, Hostilius, Diocles and me. Then he issued a curt nod and gestured for his men to retreat to a respectful distance. Soon, they had kindled a fire of their own.

Like us, Marcus had shed his blood-smeared armour and he was garbed in the simple tunic of a soldier. Apart from his bearing, the only thing that hinted at his status was the deep purple colour of his cloak.

"Claudius Germanicus", I said, and filled a wooden cup with wine which the emperor accepted with a nod. "Welcome to our hearth."

"I have learned much from Gallienus", Marcus jested. "You do the work while I am awarded the honours."

"Make no mistake, today's battle was balanced on the edge of a blade", Hostilius sighed, raising his cup to Marcus. "Many of the black riders fell to the spears of the Germani. The words you spoke inspired the men. They fought and died for you, Lord Emperor."

"And I will gladly fight and die for them and for the Empire", Marcus replied, and chugged the contents of his cup like only a soldier can.

"There is something else", Marcus said. "The barbarian champion you faced earlier today escaped during the heat of battle. The throats of the two men who guarded him were slit and his bonds cut."

"Not only did Braduhenna escape, she took her lover with her", I said.

Hostilius dismissed the unfortunate event with a wave of a hand. "It will take the Alemanni years to recover from today's defeat, and besides, the witch must have lost her credibility in the eyes of the warriors. Don't get me wrong", he added. "I would have enjoyed cutting that one's throat myself."

I did not share Hostilius's sentiments, as Braduhenna, or her predecessors in name, had proven to be a thorn in the side of Rome. But there is no use crying over spilled wine.

We were interrupted by the sound of blades sliding from scabbards as Marcus's guards drew their swords. "At ease, praetorians", the emperor commanded as three Goths appeared from the darkness.

The guards slid their *gladii* back into the sheaths.

I gestured for the barbarian noble to take a seat around the cooking fire. "You are welcome at our hearth, Lord Aldara", I said, and gestured to his oathsworn to join the praetorians, who eyed them with suspicion.

Marcus might have been the emperor, but from the point of view of the men of the tribes, I was the war chief of the Romans, the one guided by the hand of their god of war. For that reason, Aldara deferred to me.

"I have come to speak with you on a matter of great importance, Lord Eochar", the Goth commander said as he eased himself to the ground.

I nodded, indicating that I accepted his request.

"The Germani's baggage train and plundered livestock remain in the mouth of the Brenner Pass", he said. "Their wagons are loaded with the supplies that my people need to survive the coming winter."

"You have honoured your word so I will honour my oath to Tharuarus", I said. "Our scouts report that fewer than three thousand men guard the loot."

"Do you wish to lead the attack, lord?" Aldara asked.

"No", I replied. "Take your men and claim the provisions that you need for your people."

"And the Germani?" he asked.

"It would be better if the locals are not burdened with warbands of survivors who turn to brigandage", I said.

"I understand, lord", he replied, issued a smile that chilled my blood, and beckoned for his men to accompany him to their camp.

Hostilius did not notice, or if he did, it was clear that he cared little that the fate of the Alemanni guarding the baggage train appeared bleak at best. The Primus Pilus slapped his knees with open palms and came to his feet. "For the first time in many years I feel like the gods favour the Empire", he said, and raised his cup to Marcus. "We've conquered the Goths and all but crushed the Alemanni. Where do we go from here? Do we take back Gaul and Germania that Postumus stole or do we ride east to put Zenobia in her place?"

"Two months ago I would have said that a campaign is impossible, but without them realising it", Marcus mused while sipping on his wine, "the Goths and the Alemanni have done us a favour by invading Roman lands."

There were frowns all around, except for Diocles, who grasped the workings of the Empire better than most.

"Tell them, tribune", Marcus said, and gestured for my aide to elaborate.

"Emperor Claudius inherited an Empire with empty coffers", Diocles replied. "After the loss of revenue from the rich Eastern Provinces, Gaul and Germania, it did not take long for Rome to become bankrupt."

My aide took a swallow of wine, allowing the stark reality to sink in.

"The Empire cannot go to war without gold", Diocles continued. "Without coin, there is no provisions or pay for the legionaries and no feed for the draught animals."

"Why don't you just raise a war tax?" Hostilius asked.

"If I do that, what remains of the Empire will be in open revolt before the end of the month", Marcus said. "People prefer being conquered to paying higher tax."

"That was the precarious situation we found ourselves in until the Goths invaded", Marcus continued. "As we speak, wagonloads of gold and silver taken from them are on the way to the mints in the provinces", Marcus confirmed. "In addition, we took thousands of slaves that will be sold at a good profit. Great herds of cattle, horses and sheep are making their way to the markets. Soon, the treasury of the Empire will be flush with coin again."

"The Goths have taken all their plunder from Roman Provinces, is it not?" Hostilius asked Diocles. "Now that same loot is filling up the coffers in Rome?"

My aide nodded. "That is the gist of it."

"So, the savages actually collected your taxes?" the Primus Pilus concluded.

"It is as you say, tribune", Marcus confirmed. "If I had sent my tax collectors to peacefully ask for but half of what the Goths had plundered, my name would have been cursed throughout the Empire. The Goths took all that the people possessed by violence and rapine, and I, in turn, have taken it from them. The treasury still ends up with the gold, but with the difference that the name of Claudius Gothicus is honoured as the saviour of the Empire."

"In this case", Diocles interjected, "the invaders have done the Empire a favour by collecting the wealth of Raetia and Germania before delivering it to Italia."

"I have agreed with Tharuarus that he may lay claim to sufficient food and livestock to see his people through the winter", I said. "All the other plunder we have captured will go to the imperial coffers so that we may strengthen the Empire for the benefit of the people."

"I'll drink to that", Hostilius said, and chugged the contents of his cup.

I decided to change the subject.

"How goes Vibius's campaign against the Goth tribes that fled into the Haemus Mountains after their defeat at Naissus?" I asked.

"He is making slow but steady progress", Marcus said. "The errant tribes' provisions must be low and winter is around the corner. My prediction is that those who survive the cold will surrender come spring, or mayhap even sooner."

It was a reasonable assessment, but one the gods must have found amusing.

Chapter 17 – Plunder

Late morning the following day, Gordas, Hostilius, Diocles and I were training with the sword on the shores of the lake when Hlodwig arrived with news.

"Dead?" Hostilius asked after the big man had given his report, the expression on the Primus Pilus's face incredulous.

"I saw the body", Hlodwig confirmed.

"Tell us", I commanded the Frank.

"We harried the rear of the horde for the last few days as you had ordered, Lord Eochar", he said. "Each time they tried to engage we retreated up the valley. And we were careful not to show our true numbers."

Diocles passed the big man a cup of wine. He wetted his throat and continued.

"The enemy blockaded our approach", he said. "They hid behind a double line of ox wagons fortified with spears. If we had tried to break through, we would have been defeated."

"It was a wise decision, Hlodwig", I said. "Only a fool throws away the lives of his men without need."

The Frank nodded his acceptance of my words. "Then I received your message, lord. Earlier today the rest of the Goth army attacked the foe's baggage train from the southern side of the pass. Once Lord Aldara's force had managed to breach the *wagenburg*, we broke through from the north. The battle was over in less than a sixth of a watch."

"Did Aldara have a good death?" Gordas asked. "Did he die with a blade in his fist?"

"A spear pierced his heart", the Frank replied.

Gordas grunted his approval, but by the way Hlodwig averted his eyes, I suspected there was more to the story.

"There is more?" I asked.

"The Goths lost many riders when they broke through the barricade of wagons", Hlodwig explained. "Lord Aldara led from the front. It was a fierce fight."

"Did he fall during the assault on the barricade?" Diocles asked.

Hlodwig shook his head. "After the battle, Lord Aldara had words with one of his ringmen. Something spooked his horse and it reared. The Goth lord was thrown from the saddle onto the spears that the Alemanni had lashed to their wagons."

"Have they sent his shade on its way?" I asked.

"No, lord", Hlodwig replied. "The Goths were busy gathering wood for the pyres when I left."

"Come", I said. "Let us go and pay our respects to Aldara. He was a good man."

Gordas demonstrated that he understood the ways of the tribes by asking the pertinent question. "Who is the man that Aldara had words with?"

"His nephew, Little Wolf", Hlodwig replied.

* * *

Ulfilas, as the Goths called him in their tongue, had taken command of the *foederati* after the untimely demise of his uncle. I had never spoken with the young man, but I had seen him in Aldara's presence. Apparently he was a well-respected champion in his own right, a man whose arms were heavy with gold and silver.

"I am told that Little Wolf is not only good with a blade, but he has cunning as well", Hlodwig said as we approached the place where the warriors guarding the baggage train had made their last stand.

"He is the son of Tharuarus, the war chief of the Goths who led the invasion of Macedonia", the Frank added, a detail which I was not aware of.

"Given the family connection, I wonder why Tharuarus had not placed his son in command of the Goth *foederati*?" Diocles mused as he slowed his gelding to a trot.

"Don't make too much of the savages and their family connections", Hostilius said. "All the men we put to the blade yesterday were probably related to one another in some way or other. You know how these barbarians are, they breed like rabbits, so they're bound to be connected by blood."

"I have heard whispers that Lord Tharuarus does not approve of the ways of his son", Hlodwig said as we approached the stacks of wood that the Goths had gathered in order to burn the corpses of their fallen.

"We will judge for ourselves", I said, and swung down from the saddle.

* * *

We found Ulfilas overseeing the gathering of the plunder. He was still dressed in blood-spattered armour, except for his riveted helmet that hung from his saddle.

"Lord Ulfilas", I said. "Greetings."

He did not dismount, but addressed us from atop his gelding - an insult of the worst kind.

"We crushed the Germani because they are weak", the Goth commander said, and slowly closed his fist to demonstrate the action. "If you have come to claim the honour, you are too late, Roman."

Before Ulfilas had spoken two sentences, my mind was made up.

It is strange how fools and men of evil disposition covet positions of power, while honourable men are mostly reluctant to embrace command. In this case it was clear that the young Goth was a fool - only time would tell if he was evil.

"We wish to pay our respects to Lord Aldara", I said. "Before his shade departs to the warrior hall of the gods."

"You can pay all the respect you want", he sneered in the tongue of the Goths, "but Aldara did not die with a blade in his fist. You claim to walk in the shadow of Teiwaz, Roman - do you not know that the god will not welcome a man beside his hearth who fell from the saddle in a drunken stupor?" His hand dropped to the hilt of his blade to emphasize his hostile tone.

Ulfilas's words and actions convinced me that foolishness was not his only vice.

But the wicked fool commanded the twenty thousand barbarians who surrounded us. I was not about to undo our success of recent days, so I forced myself to swallow back a rebuke and gritted my teeth to suppress the red-hot anger that rose in my throat like bile.

"It is as you say, Lord Ulfilas. Teiwaz decides the fates of men", I said, and turned my back to join Hostilius, Gordas and Diocles in prayer beside the pyre where Aldara's shade was rising to the heavens.

* * *

Two days later, I sat in the saddle beside Marcus when the Goths arrived at the Roman camp to hand over our share of the loot. Behind the hundred odd wagons, I noticed thousands of barbarian horsemen.

"I have brought my men to ensure that your share of the plunder arrived safely", Ulfilas said, and gestured at the carts with a flourish that was in poor taste. It was abundantly clear that the Goth cavalry was not present to guard the treasure, but rather to intimidate us into submission. In addition, the five thousand Carpiani horse archers were not in attendance because I believe that Ulfilas was unsure of where their loyalties lay.

"Did you honour my agreement with your war chief, Tharuarus?" I asked, already knowing the answer.

"I have given you more than your fair share", Ulfilas sneered. "Do you dispute my judgement?"

Ulfilas was spoiling for a fight. I realised that he would use the slightest provocation as an excuse to unleash his men and claim the head of the emperor. On his return to the tribe, he would share the abundance of plunder amongst the nobles, and, in light of his success, be elevated to war chief.

What the Goth leader did not know was that, except for slaves and servants, the Roman camp was empty. The Illyrian horsemen were concealed within the shadows of the pine-covered slope to our right, two hundred paces distant. They waited patiently in their saddles, their lances grounded, ready to charge on my command.

I also realised that an all-out confrontation between the Illyrians and the Goths, who outnumbered us nearly three to one, would be a close-matched fight. One thing was certain though, and that was that both sides would lose many brave warriors - a situation that we wished to avoid at all cost.

Apart from laying claim to a larger part of the Germani plunder, there was another breach of the agreement - one that could not be so easily set aside.

"Where are the thousands of Roman men and women taken as slaves by the Alemanni?" I asked. "Tharuarus had agreed to free them."

"It is not my understanding of the terms", Ulfilas replied. "My people are in need of thralls."

"We will buy them from you", Marcus proposed.

"They are not for sale, but who am I to deny the emperor of Rome", he mocked. "They will not come cheap, though. Romans make excellent slaves because they are meek and obedient."

"We will exchange the prisoners for our share of the loot", Marcus suggested, his words bringing a grimace of triumph to the Goth's lips.

"It will be as you command, Lord Emperor", he said, bowed in a way that was mocking in my eyes, and thundered off, shouting commands to his men.

"We can defeat them, Lord Emperor", Hostilius asserted from my right.

Gordas issued a grunt that I took as support for the Primus Pilus.

"At what cost, tribune?" Marcus said. "This summer has seen us defeat the Goths and crush the Alemanni. Although Fortuna favoured us, she is known to be fickle. Let us be content with our victories. During the coming winter our armouries will toil to churn out spears, swords and shields. Due to our success, recruits will flock to our camps where we will train them and incorporate them into the battle-hardened legions. Come spring of next year, the armies of Rome will once again be at full strength, armed to the teeth, and ready to crush any foe foolish enough to stand in our path."

Marcus's words were wise indeed. It made me realise that my friend had become the man he was destined to be. I could not help but wonder that if it were up to me, would I have been able to restrain myself? Or would I have gambled all to slake the god of war's insatiable appetite for blood?

Chapter 18 – Family (October 269 AD)

Verona, Northern Italia.

Five weeks later.

"The Illyrians are ready to ride", I said. "The wounded have recovered and the horses are well-fed and rested."

"Good, good", Marcus said. "Any news of the Goth convoy?"

"They must be close to Siscia by now", I said. "Ulfilas may be a fool, but he knows that if his army tarries, they might not be in time to deliver the much-needed supplies to their tribe. If his people starve due to his tardiness, they will kill him when he eventually returns."

"And you are confident that he will not loot Roman farms and villages along the way?" Marcus asked, raising an eyebrow.

"Not confident enough not to have sent three hundred Illyrians east to escort them", I replied.

"Good, good", Marcus said, his tone absentminded.

I had known the emperor for more than thirty years. It was clear that he was distracted.

He dismissed me with a wave of a hand and turned away.

I stood unmoving.

"What bothers you, Lucius?" he sighed.

"I was about to ask you the same question, Lord Emperor", I replied.

Marcus scowled in reply and took a seat on a gold-inlaid divan. "Is it that obvious?" he asked.

"It is", I said, and sat down on the couch opposite.

He reached for a scroll on a low side table and unrolled the document, which he read in silence before returning it to its place. "You know that I have a half brother", he said.

I nodded, as he had told me years before of the troubled relationship between him and Quintillus.

"My brother and I cannot be more different", he said. "I am a man of the legions who does not approve of the ways of the senate. He is a man of the senate who does not approve of the ways of the legions. There is very little common ground between us."

"It has always been the case, has it not?" I said, and accepted a cup from the hand of the ruler of the known world. "Why is it bothering you all of a sudden?"

"Ever since I have taken up the purple, he has started to write to me", Marcus said, and took a slow sip from his cup. "He asked me to deliberate with the senate before I act - advice which I have ignored to date." Marcus indicated the scroll. "Now he insists on joining my retinue in a bid to strengthen the relationship between the emperor and the senators."

"Tell him to stay in Rome", I heard myself say. I must admit, my words sounded much like the Primus Pilus's to my own ears.

"You spend too much time in Hostilius's company", Marcus replied.

"I guess the Primus Pilus's advice is preferred to Gordas's wisdom", I said. "I have no doubt that the Hun would counsel you to cut Quintillus's throat as soon as he arrives."

The truth of my words made both of us grin.

"Sometimes I wish I could, but Quintillus, apart from sharing my blood, holds much sway in the senate", Marcus said. "If I refuse my brother's offer, it would sour my relationship with the conscript fathers."

I rolled my eyes at his use of the traditional name for the senate, a gesture that did not go unnoticed.

"I wish I shared your outlook, Lucius", he sighed, and took another swallow. "Then my life would have been much less complicated."

"If I were in your boots, I would ride to Rome and wade in amongst those old fools with my blade", I jested. "It would be the salvation of the Empire."

"Even a killer like you would not dare do that", Marcus replied.

I shrugged noncommittally.

Another idea came to mind. "Why not summon your brother to Sirmium and give him a taste of the life of a soldier", I suggested. "Mayhap he will find that he is not cut out to ride into battle."

A mischievous grin split Marcus's lips, but before he could reply, there was a knock at the door.

"Lord", the praetorian said. "There is an officer who wishes an audience with Legate Domitius."

Marcus indicated for the man to be allowed to be escorted in by his guards. Although the officer was covered in dust, grime, and what I believed to be specks of dried blood, I immediately recognised him as a decurion in the ranks of the

Illyrians. As soon as I laid eyes on him I knew that there was trouble afoot.

He saluted in the way of the legions and both Marcus and I reciprocated.

"Speak, decurion", I ordered.

"A few days ago, near Siscia, we led the barbarians across the stone bridge that spans the river", the decurion said.

"The Savus?" Marcus asked.

"Yes, lord", the officer replied. "We followed the river down from Neviodunum through Andautonia. We stuck to the northern road because the horses and cattle needed much watering in the heat."

"A sound strategy", Marcus said, and gestured for the man to continue.

"As you had ordered, legate, we tried to get the savages …., er, *foederati*, across the river before nightfall to make sure that they stay out of mischief. But mid-afternoon, an ox wagon lost a wheel", he said. "The axle broke as well, and only the intervention of Fortuna kept the cart from ending up in the river, oxen and all."

"Did you order the city to shut its gates?" I asked.

"We did as you had commanded, lord", the decurion said. "And the Illyrians camped inside the walls of Siscia. In the middle hour of the night, the Goths tried to breach the walls."

"Were they successful?" I asked, knowing that the walls of Siscia were not in the best state of repair.

"Two hundred of my men were patrolling the walls to bolster the local guard", he said. "We managed to beat back the attack, but lost at least fifty good soldiers."

"You did well to repel twenty thousand", Marcus said.

The decurion lowered his gaze, unwilling to accept the praise.

"It wasn't us, Lord Emperor", he said, his voice hoarse. "Come morning, the Goths came again. They threw their best men at the places where the walls were crumbling. I've been in enough skirmishes to know when all is lost, lords, so I ordered my men to make peace with their gods."

The Illyrian, clearly thirsty, started to cough.

I poured the decurion a cup of wine and indicated for him to wet his parched throat, which he did with a grateful nod.

"And then the gods of Rome intervened and made the Scythians turn on their fellow barbarians", he said. "Wave after wave of horsemen attacked the Goths from the rear."

"The Carpiani?" I asked.

He nodded. "They forgot all about taking the city and went after the Carpiani, who fled east", he said. "I ordered my men to take word to all the walled towns and settlement to the east."

"What about their wagons filled with loot?" I asked.

"The Goths left most of the provisions behind, but took all the gold and silver they could carry", the officer said.

"Make sure you and your men get food into your bellies and a good night's rest", I said as I dismissed him. "I expect you to be ready to ride come morning."

"I understand, legate, and I will obey", the decurion said, saluted, and left to do as I had ordered.

* * *

Late afternoon, we sighted the stone walls of Siscia in the distance.

During the eight days on the road, continued reports poured in from the east. Apart from the unsuccessful attempt of the Goths to breach the city's walls, and a few instances where farms bordering the road were plundered, they had focused their efforts on returning to Naissus. After his failed gamble and the revolt of the Carpiani, Ulfilas must have realised that if he ended up being caught between the Illyrians and the legions based in Naissus, things would not go well for them.

What their leader did not know was that I had no intention to engage the retreating Goths. In my eyes, Ulfilas was a rogue leader who had acted without the authority of their war chief. Why would I sacrifice the lives of thousands of Illyrians if the mistakes of Ulfilas could be rectified by sharing a horn of mead with Tharuarus?

Marcus had sent word east to warn Vibius of the approaching barbarian convoy, including orders to refrain from engaging the Goths.

"If we don't drag our feet there will still be enough light to inspect the city's walls", Hostilius observed casually.

Marcus fixed the Primus Pilus with a sidelong glance. "A good point, tribune", he said, and kicked his stallion to a strong canter.

"Best keep up with the emperor" I said, and followed suit.

* * *

As was his habit, Hortensius saved the best for last, only serving up the gossip after dessert.

The multitude of servants who, over the course of the evening, had kept our plates and goblets full, discreetly vanished moments before the innkeeper pushed open the double doors of the dining room bearing a platter heaped with iced peaches, dates and fresh figs. Behind him followed a slave carrying an ornate glass bowl filled with white wine, a layer of flower petals floating on top. "The violet wine I make myself, my lords", he boasted as he waved the woman from our presence. "The secret is to rise while it is still dark and pick only the flowers that are free from dew. Anything else is sure to spoil the delicate aromas."

I noticed Gordas raise an eyebrow. He beckoned for Hortensius to fill his goblet and chugged the contents, multi-coloured petals and all. The Hun gestured for the innkeeper to refill his cup, but our host seemed reluctant. He was about to offer an explanation when Marcus took him by the elbow and indicated that he should join us on the couches.

"After you had informed us of Postumus's demise, I sent ambassadors to Hispania", Marcus said. "Early indications are that they are keen to embrace the Empire. For us to resume trade with the Hispanic Provinces, it would be best to have a land bridge that connects Italia to Hispania."

"That would be Gallia Narbonensis and Aquitania", Diocles clarified for the sake of our host.

"Have you recently had contact with merchants from those provinces?" Marcus asked.

"Lord Emperor", Hortensius said, an expression of shock settling on his face. "Men who reside in the breakaway Gallic Empire are certainly not welcome in the Empire and by extension not at my inn."

I noticed Gordas empty another cup of violet wine, which drew a frown from our host.

"We've known each other for years. For the sake of the gods, spare us the law-abiding citizen act", Hostilius said.

A sly smile settled on Hortensius's lips and he narrowed his eyes. "Just yesterday a wealthy merchant from Massilia spent an evening at the inn", he revealed. "He is well connected with the families of Gallia Narbonensis who wield the power in the province."

Marcus gestured for him to continue.

"Years before, the powerful families in the province supported Postumus only because they despised Gallienus. Since you have taken the reins, Lord Emperor, the rulers of Narbonensis are keen to be forgiven for their, er…, indiscretions of the past."

"It is good to know", Marcus said, and sipped from his cup.

"What tidings are there from Rome?" I asked.

"Your spectacular defeat of the Alemanni overshadows everything", Hortensius said.

"We are soldiers", Hostilius asserted. "We want tidings, not flattery."

Our host leaned in, and lowered his voice to just above a whisper. "Not all in the senate are content with your victories, Lord Emperor. Word is that support for the Harbinger is waning. People wish to back an emperor who is victorious on the field of battle, an emperor who cowers Rome's enemies."

Marcus raised his cup, but before he could chug the contents Hortensius stopped him. "Violet wine is delicious", he said, "but have a care, lord, it can move the bowels strongly."

Marcus took another sip just as Gordas emptied his fourth bowl.

Chapter 19 – Naissus

Five days later, a few miles outside of Sirmium.

"It appears that you will reconquer Hispania and Southern Gaul by the strength of your reputation alone, Lord Emperor", Diocles reflected. Then he twisted in the saddle to address Hostilius. "You see, tribune, sometimes disputes can be settled without the sword."

Hostilius scoffed at my aide's words. "And how do you think the emperor gained his reputation in the first place - at the negotiating table?"

Gordas saved Diocles from having to answer the question.

"You are right, centurion", the Hun said, biting back a stomach cramp. "Through the path of blood, one's enemies must learn that once you have bared your iron, they will die. Only then do they send envoys bearing gifts who talk of peace."

"It is good to know that some of the provinces that had sided with Postumus are eager to come back into the fold of the Empire", Marcus said. "Yet, I tend to agree with Tribune Proculus and Gordas. Rome will never regain all the lost

Gallic provinces unless we put the fear of the gods into whoever rules the breakaway regions."

It was late afternoon when we eventually arrived at Sirmium, the city which the emperor had come to think of as home.

I made to enter the gates, but Marcus placed a hand on my shoulder. "You have done enough, Lucius", he said. "I wish for you and your entourage to spend a few well-deserved days with your families."

"Then let us take the Illyrians east to Naissus in three days' time", I suggested. "When we have settled matters with Tharuarus once and for all, we can return home before the snow comes."

"I fear that this winter I will spend more time at your home than mine", Marcus sighed. "I am expecting Quintillus within the month."

"The emperor of Rome is not welcome under my roof", I said, causing an expected frown to crease Marcus's brow. "But my old friend Marcus Claudius can warm himself beside my hearth whenever he so pleases", I added with a grin.

Marcus nodded and led his victorious army to the gates of Sirmium, while Hostilius, Gordas, Diocles and I nudged our mounts to a canter, eager to be reunited with friends and family.

* * *

"Ulfilas is a bigger problem than you think", Segelinde said while I lay in her arms later that evening.

"He is but a young fool who wants to make a name for himself", I replied. "I will speak with his father, Tharuarus, who will rein him in."

"You need to kill him, and you need to do it soon", she said, her voice suddenly cold. "Do not make the same mistake Kniva made. If my brother had hunted down the Crow, he would still be the king of the Goths. Mercy is just another word for weakness."

"Ulfilas is the son of the war chief", I said. "I cannot just walk into their camp and cut his throat."

"That's not what I said, husband", she said. "But if he gives you the slightest reason, challenge him, and kill him. If you show him mercy, you will regret it."

* * *

Three days later, Hostilius, Diocles and I completed the short ride to Sirmium. Although the sun was yet to rise, we found Marcus at the head of the Illyrians outside the gates of the city. The Roman horsemen were in formation and ready to ride east.

"It is good to have a proper emperor for a change", Hostilius said once we had fallen in with Marcus's retinue. "If it were Gallienus, he would have stumbled from his chambers sometime after midday, demanding to be carried in a litter."

I studied Marcus. Although he was not a young man, he was still a formidable warrior.

Diocles noticed my musings. "I understand why the senate fear him so", he said. "Never has the Empire had a ruler with a mind as sharp as his blade. It has always been one or the other."

"History will remember his name", I replied. "He will be known as one of the greatest."

On Marcus's command, the wolf-cloaked signifer raised the imperial standard. In response, the column of horsemen started east, headed for the lair of the Goths.

***

A slave bearing a leather satchel added a handful of lavender seeds to each of the four braziers that were strategically positioned near the corners of the chamber. Once done, he bowed low, shuffled backwards, and closed the double doors behind him to keep the pleasant scent from escaping the stone room in the fort at Naissus.

"So?" Marcus asked Vibius. "Have you finished off the last of the errant barbarian warbands?"

A hurt expression settled on my friend's face. "I know better than that", he said. "When the Sasanian royals hunt bears, the warriors riddle the poor thing with arrows but refrain from striking the killing blow."

"Why is that?" Hostilius asked, and slurped at his cup of heated wine.

"They pin down the beast until their king comes cantering along in all his splendour to pierce the bear's heart with his lance", Vibius explained. "The glory always belongs to the *shahanshah*."

"And am I right to assume that the Goth bear is trembling on its last legs, riddled by your arrows?" Marcus asked.

"Of course, Lord Emperor", our friend affirmed. "All that remains is for you to pierce the beast's chest with your gilded spear."

There was a lull in the conversation as the head of the imperial kitchen entered. He was followed by a servant carrying a tray of wooden bowls filled with steaming pottage. "Bean and beef broth as you ordered, Lord Emperor", the cook said, indicating for the bowls to be placed on a low table.

The man's gaze settled on the simple fare which would not have been out of place at the dinner table of peasants. "I have prepared a second course of asparagus pie with lovage and pepper accompanied by elderberry custard", he said. "It is more suited to your status, lord."

Marcus fixed the man with a glare. "Was I not clear in my instructions?"

"I apologise, Lord Emperor", the cook said, swallowed nervously, and backpedalled from the room.

"What use is asparagus pie to a soldier?" Marcus sighed. "Where were we?"

"You had just arrived with your gilded lance", Vibius said with a mischievous grin. "All jests aside", he continued, "the campaign against the Goths has been difficult. Many thousands of barbarians sought refuge in the foothills of the Haemus Mountains. From there they sent warbands out to forage for food and loot. We hunted these warbands with mixed success, but I believe that we have them cornered. Many will not survive the coming winter."

"Any word of Thiaper and the Carpiani?" I asked. "We will have to supply them with provisions as they've had a falling out with the Goths."

"They must have made camp somewhere to the south", Vibius shrugged.

A sudden gush rattled the closed shutters, and I reached for a fur cloak draped over the backrest of the couch.

"There will be snow soon", I said.

"Cai", I asked, addressing the Easterner who sat beside me. "Did you manage to coax Tharuarus back to health?"

"You still lot to learn, Lucius of Da Qin", Cai said. "Body heal itself."

"So, did Tharuarus manage to heal himself?" Hostilius asked offhandedly, and took another sip from his cup.

"Yes", Cai replied.

"I will visit the Goth war leader tomorrow. There is no doubt in my mind that he will accept the provisions that they left behind at Siscia in return for peace", I said. "Would you care to join us, Vibius?"

"Actually, I was planning on asking Tribune Hostilius and Diocles to lend me a hand", Vibius replied.

"With what?" Hostilius asked, and took another gulp from his cup.

"I require your skills to track down an elusive warband of Peucini Goths who are terrorizing the lands to the south", Vibius replied. "We will be leading two cohorts of legionaries."

Heavy infantry was the Primus Pilus's first love. It was clear that he was keen to accept the invitation. "Do you think you can stay out of trouble this one time, Domitius?" he asked. "Or do you want me and the Greek to hold your hand?"

"I will keep him safe", Gordas replied.

* * *

One of the two Goth axemen guarding the war chief's tent pushed aside the felt flap and disappeared into the smoke-filled interior. The other eyed us warily, his right fist clasped around the thick haft in a vice-like grip.

The first ringman returned and grunted something unintelligible to his comrade. Then they lowered their whetted blades and stepped to the side. "Only you, lord", the guard stated while fixing me with his eyes.

"I will speak with the war chief in private", I said to Gordas.

"Expect treachery", he whispered in the togue of the Huns, his deep-seated distrust of the Goths almost palpable.

I ducked into the gloom, pausing inside to allow my eyes to adjust to the low light.

Beside the blazing hearth at the centre of the tent sat two men - Tharuarus, the war chief, and his son Ulfilas, the fool. Unlike me, they wore no armour, only tunics with thick furs draped around their shoulders. I had come in the name of the Empire and I was dressed in the war gear of a Roman general.

"You are welcome at my hearth, Lord Eochar", Tharuarus said, and indicated that I should join them. Ulfilas's eyes were cast down, staring into the fire. I wondered why.

"My son has told me about the campaign", Tharuarus said, and gestured for a slave to pass me an ale horn before waving the girl from our presence.

I nodded, but wondered what lies he had told his father.

"Ulfilas speaks highly of you, Lord Eochar", Tharuarus said, and took a long swig from his horn. "He says that Romans and Goths fight well together."

It took all my restraint to not choke on my ale, but I managed to control my surprise. "Your son is wise, indeed", I replied, my words bringing a look of pride to the father's eyes.

"In his eagerness to ensure the survival of the tribe, my son foolishly laid claim to a larger share of the plunder than what was his due", the war chief said. "He has seen the error of his ways. Wagons filled with gold and silver will soon be delivered to the Roman fort at Naissus."

I had prepared myself for difficult negotiations. Tharuarus's meekness took the wind from my sails, leaving me at a loss for words. "You honour me, lord", I said. "In return, I will ensure that the sufficient provisions are delivered to your camp to feed your people during the cold season."

All raised their cups, toasting the agreement.

The war chief placed an oaken arm around the shoulders of his son. "Little Wolf tells me that you defeated a champion in single combat."

"It is as Ulfilas says", I replied, still off-balance.

"Is it true that your blade is crafted from sky-iron that was cast down to earth by the gods?" Tharuarus asked, his eyes wide.

My sword had achieved legendary status, and I knew that there were few men that would not give their front teeth to hold the blade in their fist.

"Do you wish to see it?" I asked.

A smile split the headman's bearded face and he issued a curt nod.

I passed the blade hilt first to Tharuarus, who reverently tested its balance. "It truly is a magnificent weapon", he said, and laid it on his open palms.

I leaned forward to accept the sword, but Ulfilas interjected. "May I, Lord Eochar?" he asked.

Ulfilas's words made me change my perception of the young Goth. In a clever ploy he had managed to disarm me - mayhap he was no fool after all. I could not refuse the young man without insulting him, and even worse, incur the wrath of his father.

"You may", I replied, and I leaned back. If Little Wolf planned treachery, at least I would be out of reach of a swipe from my own blade. In addition, I reached underneath my fur cloak, my right hand finding the hilt of my dagger. Every sinew in my body was as tight as a newly braided bowstring as the young Goth's fist closed around the pommel of my sword. A broad grin split his lips as he tested the balance and savoured the lightness of the blade. Then the iron cleft the air in a silver blur.

I jumped up into a crouch, my dagger ready to repel the thrust.

But the strike was not meant for me.

Eyes wide, Tharuarus clutched at the blade buried deep in his heart. "S... Son?" he stammered with his last breath.

"You are not my father, coward", Ulfilas spat as the corpse slowly toppled onto its back. "You lacked the courage to fight to the death and willingly bent the knee to our mortal enemies."

Then Ulfilas turned his gaze on me and slid his iron from the scabbard, a sly smile splitting his thin lips. "Treachery! Treachery!" he boomed.

Chapter 20 – Little Wolf

I harboured no illusions about what the guards would believe when they saw my iron buried to the hilt in the chest of Tharuarus. I placed my boot on the dead war chief's torso and retrieved the weapon in a spray of red, just as the two axemen stormed into the pavilion.

The Goth nearest to me swung his war axe like a farmer wielding a scythe, intent on chopping me in half. I lunged to get inside the arc of the blade, the haft of his weapon striking the boiled leather strips of my skirt at the same instant that I rammed my dagger into the unprotected base of his neck.

From the corner of my eye, I noticed Little Wolf cutting with his longsword, the edge flashing from high to low. I was left with no option but to turn my back to the second guard and deflect the power of Ulfilas's strike. The ringman's blade ripped scales from my armour, and I felt the familiar sting as the iron drew blood.

I steeled myself for the impact of the second guard's axe, but instead I heard a gasp followed by a scream in the tongue of the Goths as Gordas's battle-axe crushed the skull of the man intent on striking me from behind.

Suddenly outnumbered, Ulfilas used the brief respite to sweep his blade across the leather at the far side of the tent and ducked through the slit.

I thought on Segelinde's words and made to follow the Goth, but Gordas grabbed my arm in a grip of iron. "They come, Eochar", he said. "There are too many, you cannot kill them all."

Gordas pushed the flap aside and we peeked at the camp that, in the space of fifty heartbeats, had fallen into chaos. Warriors were shouting warnings of treachery, reaching for their blades. Others were fitting armour or calling their fellows to arms.

"It is now or never", I said.

Gordas led the way, sprinting to where our horses were tethered. In one motion, he slashed both reins free with his dagger and vaulted onto the back of his mare. I gained the saddle in a manoeuvre that would have brought a smile to the Hun's lips had he seen it.

Gordas dug his heels into the flanks of his mount. Before the horse could react, a burly warrior burst from between two tents and rammed his spear into the mare's neck. The horse whinnied in pain, stumbled, and went to ground. My friend somehow avoided being crushed by his mount, but his attacker was not as fortunate. In a last act of defiance, the horse fell on top of the Goth.

Gordas landed on his feet like a feline, crouching beside the mare. Without concern for his own wellbeing, he removed his helmet and reached out to gently stroke the neck of the dying animal while he whispered words in the tongue of the Huns. Seemingly in a trance, Gordas paid no heed to the Goth warriors who came rushing through the gaps between the tents and wagons.

Like a vice, I clamped my legs against Kasirga's sides, reached down from the saddle, gripped the Hun's armour at the neck, and allowed the power of my horse to jerk my friend to his feet. "Jump!" I boomed, ignoring the pain that shot through my shoulder.

Gordas added his effort to that of my horse and landed on my stallion's back, just in front of the saddle.

Another spear cleft the air and struck me a glancing blow from behind, but my armour turned the iron and saved my life.

Kasirga must have sensed the urgency and was at a gallop in fewer than five heartbeats. Three spear-wielding warriors tried to block our path, but my enormous warhorse crashed through their barricade, spinning their broken bodies to the side and crushing what remained beneath his hooves.

And then we were free from the sea of tents, and Kasirga lengthened his stride. I glanced over my shoulder and noticed mounted men pouring from the barbarian camp.

"Our death won't be quick if we fall into the clutches of the Goth scum", Gordas said. "They will flay us alive before they use fire."

"They will not catch us", I said with more confidence than I felt.

The Hun twisted his body to look at the hundreds of riders trailing us by three hundred paces. "Kasirga is a prince amongst horses, but even he won't make it back to the Roman camp with two riders wearing armour", he said.

For a span of heartbeats Gordas said naught, but when he spoke his voice was thick with emotion. "I have had a good life, Eochar", he said, and by his tone I knew that he was saying farewell and about to sacrifice himself.

"We die together, my friend, or we survive together", I growled in the tongue of the Sea of Grass.

"No", he replied, and I could tell that his mind was made up.

I was not about to let the Hun have his way. Before he could jump from the saddle, I plucked my dagger from its sheath and struck him against the temple with the hilt. I felt his body go limp and clamped my arm around his torso to keep him from falling.

Our pursuers knew that the man who reddened his blade would win the favour of the new war leader and the respect of the tribe. Eager for the honour, they chased us down like a pack of hounds baying for the blood of a lone wolf. With every stride their shouts came closer until I was sure that they trailed us by less than fifty paces.

I refrained from looking over my shoulder, but concentrated my efforts on praying to Arash and keeping a grip on my unconscious friend.

Gordas issued a groan that caused me to shift in the saddle. My eye caught movement near the summit of a low hill on the northern slope of the shallow valley. I squinted into the afternoon sun, just in time to spy the rear end of a horse disappear over the crest. There was no mistaking the black tail and the grey-gold rump.

Only one tribe favoured dun horses. I gambled all on one last roll of the dice. Leaning forward, I stroked Kasirga's neck with my free hand. "Just one last uphill, boy", I whispered into his ear.

My stallion powered up the hill, his lungs pumping like bellows, mouth white with foam and skin slick with sweat. But the shouts of the Goths grew ever nearer.

And then we crested the rise.

Below us, at the bottom of the valley beside a narrow waterway, lay the sprawling camp of the Carpiani. The scout I had spied earlier had probably raised the alarm, and wave after wave of Scythian horsemen poured from the settlement.

I closed my eyes to thank the god of war for the deliverance, but then it dawned on me that, in the eyes of the Carpiani, it might appear as if I was leading an attack on their camp. I had no leafy green branch at hand, but reached for the pouch attached to my saddle and raised my strung horn bow high in the air.

The Scythians were not deterred.

The ramshorn relayed commands, and thousands of shafts rose into the afternoon sky, blotting out the sun. The arrows raced to the top of their arc, slowed, and then accelerated towards their targets.

"I lied", I whispered to Kasirga when I realised that we were heartbeats from death. "One more time."

My stallion pulled his ears tight against his head. He powered ahead until the ground beneath his hooves flashed past in a blur of green. I covered Gordas's body with mine, but Fortuna intervened and the storm of arrows missed us by less than a horse length. Judging by the screams of men and their mounts, the shafts slammed into the ranks of the Goths who must have been only paces behind.

The wail of the ramshorn echoed from the slopes and another volley of death left the horn bows of the Carpiani. Kasirga had no more to give and he stumbled to a halt, swaying on his hooves. I closed my eyes, extended my open palms to the side, and prayed to the god of war and fire while I waited for the inevitable.

No iron pierced my armour.

Thousands of hooves thundered past, but one rider reined in.

I opened my eyes.

"It appears that you have fallen out with the Goths, Legate Domitius", the man said.

I stole a glance over my shoulder at the Scythians who were riddling the last of the survivors with their arrows. "I believe that you are right, King Thiaper", I replied.

* * *

On our way back to the Roman fort at Naissus, Gordas remained silent, quietly brooding.

I knew that I had greatly insulted his honour, but it was by choice and not something that could be undone. For that reason, I allowed him to resolve the matter in his own mind without issuing idle words that would mean little to a man like him.

Five miles from the Carpiani camp, the Hun reined in and swung down from the saddle.

Out of respect, I followed suit.

Even though Gordas was my friend, he was still a feral creature who had no qualms to spill blood. With his lips curled up in a snarl, his hand dropped to the hilt of his blade.

In response I opened my palms.

The people who call the unforgiving steppes their home rarely apologise. In the culture of the Sea of Grass, only cowards and weaklings try to avoid the consequences of their actions by mere words. I was neither.

For at least two hundred heartbeats Gordas faced me, his fist clamped around the hilt of his blade. Then the snarl faded from his lips and his hand left the pommel.

"We will not speak of this again, my friend", he growled.

I kept his gaze. "I will do it again if I have to", I replied.

"I know", he sighed as he gained the saddle. "It is your Roman blood."

Chapter 21 – Equal (December 269 AD)

"I knew it", Hostilius sighed. "I leave you two alone just once and you manage to get yourselves into a proper mess."

"How did you come by that bump on your head?" Marcus asked Gordas.

The Hun's ire had not fully dissipated so I answered on his behalf. "He was about to sacrifice himself for me", I said, "but was struck on the head in the process."

Gordas fixed me with a sidelong glance and issued a guttural grunt that all present chose to take as confirmation of my words.

"My scouts tell me that Ulfilas's Goths have retreated into the dales higher up in the foothills of the Mountains", Marcus said. "Once the snow arrives, it will be almost impossible to go after them."

"It also means that they will be trapped there until spring", Diocles said.

"Mayhap we can take ship for Rome", Marcus sighed. "It will give me the opportunity to silence the voices of dissent within the senate."

"Your victories are still fresh in the minds of the populace", Diocles said. "Under the circumstances you might find that the senators are pliable to your will, Lord Emperor. They will be eager to be associated with the man who is conquering one enemy after another."

"Take a legion or two with you, that's my advice", Hostilius suggested. "Just in case you find that your reputation isn't quite enough." The Primus Pilus narrowed his eyes. "Truth be told, I have a few old scores to settle so I wouldn't mind burying my iron in their flabby jowls."

I noticed Diocles nodding his head in support of Hostilius - a sign that my aide had not forgotten his suffering at the hands of an assassin in the pay of the Roman elite.

"That will not be necessary, Tribune Proculus", Marcus said, waving away the Primus Pilus's suggestion. "Besides, we need the legions to be near Naissus. When the snow melts, Ulfilas's Goths will be hungry - not only for food, but also for revenge."

There was a knock at the door and the duty tribune entered the room. "Lord Emperor", he said. "A document arrived by courier from Sirmium."

Marcus indicated for Diocles to accept the scroll on his behalf. My aide was a fast reader, but even he took at least two hundred heartbeats to scrutinise the lengthy message.

"Your brother, Quintillus, and his entourage have arrived in Sirmium, Lord Emperor", Diocles said while rolling up the scroll. "He eagerly awaits your company."

A frown creased Marcus's brow, confused at the abruptness of Diocles's summary. "Is that all?"

"Your brother has a gift for using many words to say very little, lord", Diocles replied.

Marcus gestured for my aide to fill his cup. "It seems that we will not be going to Rome after all", he sighed. "Because Rome has come to Sirmium."

***

Three weeks hence, with iron-grey skies threatening another storm, we departed.

A vicious blizzard had closed the passes days before, leaving Naissus cut off from the camps of the Carpiani and Goths.

The good news was that a large contingent of Illyrians, who had remained in Macedonia subsequent to the seaborne invasion of the Heruli, had returned days before the storm. Once again the black-clad horsemen were at full strength.

The Naissus Valley, unlike the surrounding Haemus mountains, was fertile and received little snow even amid the cold season. The abundance of water and grazing made it ideal for the Illyrians and their mounts to remain at the fort. We decided to allow the legions to return to their home bases. A single legion would remain at Singidunum while another would be stationed along the lower Danube, specifically to deter the Crow and his army from crossing the river. The battle against the enormous Goth army had resulted in many Roman deaths. An even greater number of soldiers sustained debilitating injuries that would prevent them from ever lifting a blade again. Returning to their home forts would not only provide us with the opportunity to draft recruits into the ranks, but it would also deter barbarian tribes north of the river from raiding Roman lands - or so we thought at the time.

Vibius eyed the seemingly endless column of legionaries marching in double formation. "They are exhausted after the campaign against the Goths", he said, "but they are in excellent spirits. They will be welcomed home as heroes."

Hostilius nodded his agreement. "I've walked in their shoes, just like you and Domitius", he said. "Sure, hardship is never easy to endure, but it is the bitter taste of defeat that breaks the spirit. A few months of good food, good wine and good women and they'll be champing at the bit to get stuck in again, even if they've got to march halfway across the Empire."

Marcus raised an eyebrow. "Are you suggesting that we should embark on a campaign against Zenobia of Palmyra?" he asked.

"I was speaking figuratively, of course, Lord Emperor", the Primus Pilus replied. "But now that you mention it, I wouldn't mind marching east to put that cow in her place."

"I, too, am keen to incorporate the eastern provinces into the Empire once again", Marcus said. "Once we have dealt with the Goth uprising, we will start planning the campaign."

"I can't wait", Hostilius said. "But I must confess, it will be good to spend a few weeks at home."

We were all excited about the task that lay before us, but we also shared the Primus Pilus's desire to spend a quiet winter at home in the company of family and friends.

* * *

The journey to Singidunum was an uneventful but miserable affair of rain, snow and mud that I prefer not to recount. Eventually, eight days after leaving Naissus, on a bitterly cold morning, we departed from the massive legionary fortress, heading for Sirmium.

"I can't say I'm sad to see the back of the legions", Hostilius said as we trotted through the gates. He pointed at the clear sky overhead. "From here on it's all downhill and good weather. We will be home before the sun sets tomorrow evening."

Gordas gestured at the mounted praetorians that surrounded Marcus. "If it were Octar of the Huns, you would have slept beside your women tonight", he said. "No matter what the weather."

Even the praetorians were keen to get home, so we made good time. We reached Bassiana before dark and spent a night in the comfort of the residence of the local magistrate before embarking on the final leg of our return journey to Sirmium.

Our column consisted of five hundred Illyrians and a cohort of mounted praetorians, so we had little to fear from the brigands who had come to infest the area during the decline of the Empire. But we have been soldiers most of our lives and, more out of habit than necessity, we employed scouts to ensure that we did not encounter any surprises, no matter how insignificant.

Mid-morning, shortly after watering the horses, one of the advance scouts came thundering down the Roman road. Hostilius, Gordas and I rode ahead to meet the man who clearly had something to report. "Legate", he said, saluted, and pointed in the direction he had come from. "A large column of horsemen, mayhap five hundred, are approaching. They are five miles down the road and wear the garb of praetorians."

"Show me", I said.

We followed the scout to the summit of a low rise where he reined in. A few hundred paces down the track, an orderly column of praetorians was advancing at a leisurely pace. At the head of the group rode a man dressed in the armour of a Roman general. The signifer beside him carried the banner of the Roman Senate.

"The gods help us", the Primus Pilus mumbled.

I nudged my horse to a trot with Gordas and Hostilius following close behind. We reined in fifty paces in front of the riders who had not reacted to our presence at all. Eventually the legate whispered commands to the signifer, who issued a series of notes on the *buccina* that caused the riders to rein in. Eight men detached from the ranks. Six hulking praetorians and the standard bearer escorted the immaculately dressed officer.

"Legate", I said, and inclined my head in greeting as the group halted five paces in front of us.

I was not garbed in my official dress and the officer did not return the greeting, but was kind enough to provide us with his credentials. "I am Senator Marcus Aurelius Claudius Quintillus, the brother of Imperator Caesar Marcus Aurelius Claudius Augustus."

I was no stranger to the arrogance of the senatorial elite. Quintillus was not my problem, but a burden for Marcus to bear. Antagonising his brother would not serve any purpose. "Senator", I said, and inclined my head again.

"Who are you and why are you and your auxiliary rabble barring our way?" he barked.

"I am Legate Lucius Domitius", I replied. "Commander of the imperial legions loyal to Emperor Claudius."

For a moment Quintillus was unsure of how to respond. "Well... er, legate, I need to speak with my brother on an issue of great importance."

"If you would follow us senator, I will escort you to the presence of the emperor", I said.

Quintillus nodded and gestured for us to lead the way.

Marcus's signifer issued the command to halt as soon as they laid eyes on us.

I trotted ahead and bowed my head to my friend. "Lord Emperor, your brother, Senator Marcus Aurelius Claudius Quintillus wishes to speak with you on a matter of great importance."

A slight scowl of irritation flashed across Marcus's face, no doubt due to my feigned formality, but he managed to keep his composure. "Very well, Legate Domitius", he replied.

Not wishing to be part of the proceedings, I led Hostilius and Gordas to where Diocles waited at the rear of the emperor's entourage.

I saw Quintillus dismount and go down onto one knee before Marcus, who, in turn, swung down from the saddle and raised his brother to his feet in an embrace.

"This posturing makes me sick to the stomach", Hostilius hissed. "And why in hades did that pansy call us auxiliaries?"

Marcus and Quintillus gained their saddles and the column went to a trot while the two brothers exchanged words. I noticed Marcus stiffen. He raised a hand to silence his brother and twisted around, his eyes searching until I met his gaze. I realised that my friend required my counsel and I needed no further encouragement. "Come", I said. "The Emperor calls for us."

"Repeat what you said to me, brother", Marcus said as we joined them, and there was no mistaking the iron in his voice.

Quintillus swallowed nervously. "I received word that some savages crossed the frozen Danube into Roman lands", he said. "They even tried to deceive me. A horse barbarian arrived with a message for the emperor. Can you believe how tame they have become - a lowlife wishing an audience with the emperor of Rome", he snickered.

"Which tribe was he from and what was the message?" I asked.

"Some Scythian tribe or other", he replied offhandedly.

"Roxolani maybe?" Marcus asked.

"Yes, yes", Quintillus replied. "Roxolani. The barbarian said that the northern savages had attacked them and that they cannot shield Rome from the Vandali."

My stomach constricted when he uttered the words.

"Imagine a troop of useless clansmen protecting the borders of the mighty Empire", he said. "But have no fear, I dispatched a cohort of legionaries stationed at Sirmium to deal with the threat."

"The tribes that dwell in the highlands north of the plains ruled by the Scythians are a base and savage race", I said. "They scratch out a living from digging iron from the mountains and pay tribute to the Roxolani for crossing their lands to barter their ore. My daughter and Naulobates will have their hands full if they are forced to repel an invasion of the Cotini and Osii."

"For years, the Vandali refrained from crossing the Danube, mostly because they fear to be caught on the plains by the Roxolani horse archers. With the Scythians occupied in the north, the route to Roman lands lies wide open. The Vandali can field eight thousand warriors, mayhap twice that number if they have persuaded other tribes to fight by their side."

The time for niceties was over. "In all likelihood, your brother has sent a cohort to their deaths, Marcus", I said. "If it is a full-scale invasion, even a legion will not be enough to stand against them."

The emperor's brow furrowed with concern. "I give you full imperial authority", he said, and handed me his ivory baton. "Do what you can to remedy the situation. All the men we have are at your disposal."

I turned to Diocles. "Draft orders for the legion at Singidunum to mobilise without delay. They are to march to Sirmium when the sun rises tomorrow."

"I understand legate and I will obey", Diocles said, already reaching for his stylus.

"I will take the Illyrians and the praetorians west", I said to Marcus. "Join us if you wish."

"Why do you speak to the emperor as if he is your equal?" Quintillus derided me. "Know your place, peasant."

"I advise you to hold your tongue, brother", Marcus snapped. "When it comes to making war, Lucius Domitius knows no equal."

Chapter 22 – Bloodshed

We watered the horses near the track that led into the hills north of Sirmium. Cai walked his mount closer and gestured at the path that meandered up the valley. "I go to women and children", he said. "I not wish to be part of bloodshed."

Although Cai's skills with a blade were unsurpassed, men who follow the way of the Dao are never keen to spill blood.

The Easterner had hardly started up the path when I noticed a frown of concern creasing Quintillus's brow. "What did the servant mean by bloodshed?" the emperor's brother asked.

"We will most probably engage with the Vandali", Marcus said as calmly as if announcing that he would be taking a stroll to the forum.

Quintillus's arrogant demeanour changed suddenly and drastically when he realised that we were riding into battle. Initially he tried to extract himself from the predicament, but Marcus would hear nothing of it. "You will fight by my side", Marcus said. "There is only one honour greater than to serve the emperor in life and that is to die for one's emperor."

Late afternoon, eight miles northwest of Sirmium on the road to Cibalae, we came across the place where the Roman cohort that Marcus's brother had sent east had made their last stand. They had been slaughtered to a man, and the corpses stripped of anything of value, which meant that most of the bodies lay naked in the snow beside the Roman road.

We walked amongst the dead, inspecting the carnage. On the opposite side of the track, Quintillus, surrounded by his six closest guards, rid himself of his most recent meal.

Gordas dismounted and kneeled beside a body that bore no wounds apart from a neck twisted at an unnatural angle. He pressed an open palm against a cheek of the corpse. "This one's still warm", the Hun said, his tone casual, and walked to where a horse had deposited manure. He picked up a piece and rubbed the substance between his thumb and forefinger. "These men still drew breath a third of a watch ago", he said, and pointed at tracks at the side of the cobbles. "Two, maybe three thousand Vandali - fewer than half a dozen are mounted."

Marcus looked at me for guidance because he realised that few Romans knew the ways of the barbarians as well as I.

My eyes washed over the six hundred dead Romans, and I felt the anger stir in the pit of my stomach. Slowly, it rose like bile in my throat.

"The Vandali who destroyed the cohort will be one of many warbands sent out from a central camp", I ventured. "They are on foot and will be encumbered by six hundred sets of Roman armour as well as weapons and clothes." I gestured to the corpses. "Come, let us ride them down so that our fallen may enter the afterlife with the knowledge that their deaths have been avenged."

The sun was a handspan above the western horizon when Gordas reined in where a lesser dirt track meandered up a gentle slope across a snow-covered field. "The raiders are less than a mile away", the Hun said while he slipped the loop of a sinew string over the horn nock of his lopsided bow.

We trotted up the path and dismounted twenty paces from the crest, seeking the cover of shrubs at the side of the track before attempting to find out what was on the other side of the hill.

Half a mile away, a mob of Vandali were sauntering along a flat expanse. I could hear their laughter echo across the frozen land, still elated by the easy slaughter and rich pickings.

"What is your plan?" Marcus asked, his brother standing beside him like a chastised hound seeking the goodwill of its owner.

"We cross the ridge and kill them all", I said.

Quintillus's nerves must have gotten the better of his judgement. "That is not a plan", he squirmed, his voice like that of a petulant child's. "It is suicide. The savages outnumber us two to one. Did you not see what they did to the cohort?"

Marcus gained the saddle and hefted his lance. "Come Quintillus, let us find out what the gods have ordained."

There are few things as intimidating for infantry as facing a cavalry charge on open ground. With my own eyes I had seen ranks of battle-hardened legionaries who possessed iron discipline disintegrate in the face of such an attack.

The five hundred Illyrians led the assault, the mounted praetorians following close behind. I rode in the front rank beside Marcus, Hostilius, Vibius and Diocles. We had already lowered our spears when a Vandali at the rear of the mob glanced over his shoulder and noticed the feared black riders of Rome thundering down upon them. The Illyrians rode boot-to-boot in a near-perfect line, their black lacquered shields hefted and the whetted blades of their long, armour-piercing lances glittering in the afternoon sun.

It took the barbarian warrior almost two heartbeats to close his bearded maw before he cast aside the loot he was carrying and forced his way through the ranks, screaming warnings as he went.

Even if the Vandali were disciplined, they would not have had enough time to organise themselves. To a man they discarded their plunder and scattered across the plain to avoid the terrible fate bearing down upon them. The handful of mounted nobles amongst them spurred their horses, callously riding down their own warriors too slow to scamper from their paths.

I dropped Kasirga's reins, took four arrows in my draw hand, pulled the fletching to my ear, and released the first shaft. Five heartbeats later, the three-bladed iron tip of a Hun arrow slammed into the back of the lead rider's skull, throwing him from his horse as if hit by a war hammer. My next shaft hit an oathsworn in the lower back, split his mail and pierced his spine. His horse swerved as his dying body spasmed, careening into the last remaining rider who had already slumped forward with Gordas's red-fletched arrow protruding from his neck.

Like a dark wave breaking onto a beach at night, the Illyrians spilled over the fleeing Vandali. Hundreds of the adversaries died at the end of Roman lances, while others were either crushed by the hooves of horses or cut down by the *spathas* of the praetorians. By the time the charge ground to a bloody halt deep into the barbarian ranks, we had evened the odds.

Preparing for close quarters work, the Illyrians abandoned their lances in the corpses of their victims and reached for their flanged maces. Hostilius hefted his heavy boar spear while Marcus and Diocles drew swords.

A well-armoured screaming Vandali ran at me from the side, his spear levelled, intent on driving the leaf-shaped blade through my leg to pin me to my horse. I sent a shaft through the riveted plates of his helmet and the corpse spun to the side. Beside me, I noticed Hostilius fend off two attackers with his spear. In quick succession I sent them on their way to the afterlife.

Pace by pace we carved a path of blood through the Vandali. I could not help but notice that Quintillus, still surrounded by his men, was a few paces behind Marcus, his face contorted with fear. He clutched his priceless *spatha*, the blade still shiny and unstained.

Having expended my arrows, I drew my sword.

I waded into the remaining enemies, making sure to keep Marcus in sight. I dispatched another Germani, my blade cutting deep into his neck, and stole a glance to my left to ensure that the emperor was safe. Quintillus, who was still behind Marcus, hefted his blade. For a moment I believed that he would strike at his brother, but then I spied a Vandali running at the emperor from the rear. A blow from a hoof must have rendered the warrior unconscious during our earlier charge as he wore no helmet and the one side of his face was stained with clotted blood.

The large, black-bearded brute swung his longsword at Quintillus's leg. Fortuna favoured the emperor's brother and his clumsy parry managed to deflect the blade, which cut deep into a horn of his saddle. The attacker tried to free the weapon, but the senator swiped at his head, causing him to relinquish his sword and stumble back, falling over a body in the process.

Noticing that I was distracted, a Vandali warrior ran at me with an axe. Hostilius hefted his spear to impale the warrior, but Diocles dispatched the barbarian with a perfectly timed cut which drew a nod of respect from the Primus Pilus.

I spied the black-bearded warrior regain his feet and draw a dagger with a vicious curved blade. The senator slashed frantically at the Vandali, who ducked beneath a swipe and jumped at his victim, eager to bury his blade in the chest of the Roman.

My battle-axe cleft the air and the iron spike slammed into the back of the Vandali's skull, killing him instantly and splattering grey matter all over Quintillus's face.

It was easy to tear my eyes away from the vomiting man. With a sigh, I slashed my blade across the throat of another barbarian.

Chapter 23 – Tether

Early evening, I sat with Marcus, Hostilius, Vibius and Quintillus in the emperor's residence inside the walls of Sirmium. Gordas was toiling in the stables, readying our horses for the trip to the farm, while Diocles was penning the official report of the day's happenings.

The Primus Pilus wore an expression of bored impatience similar to the looks one sees on the faces of legionaries waiting for the *buccina* to signal the end of assembly. Uncharacteristically he dismissed a pouring slave with a wave of a hand. "What in hades is holding up the scouts?" he asked. "They should have reported at least a third of a watch ago."

"Maybe the Vandali killed them all", Quintillus croaked, and proceeded to chug his wine before he gestured for the pourer to pass him the cup that Hostilius had declined.

Soon after, the duty tribune arrived at the door with a decurion in tow. "Lord Emperor", he said. "I have brought the scout as you commanded."

The scout officer saluted.

"Report, decurion", Marcus said.

"The invaders have set up a large camp, just like you said they would, Legate Domitius", the decurion confirmed. "Beside the tents of the Vandali we have seen the boar standards of the Buri and the black banners of the Lugii."

"How many?" Marcus asked.

"At least twelve thousand, lord", the decurion said. "But more savages are still arriving from the north."

Marcus made to dismiss the man, but I could see that he had more to report.

"Give us your thoughts, decurion", I said.

"The barbarians have made their camp not on Roman soil, but north of the Danube, lord", he replied.

"Thank the gods", Quintillus sighed, and drained his cup for the second time in the space of sixty heartbeats.

Marcus waved away the decurion and turned to face Quintillus. "Why are you thankful to the gods, Brother?" he asked.

"The Vandali are camped north of the Danube, which place them outside of Roman territory", the senator explained. "Strictly speaking they are not invaders if they have not crossed the river."

Vibius started to interject, but Quintillus raised a palm. "Allow me to finish, tribune", he said, his tone suddenly arrogant. "The warband we destroyed today must have been acting of their own accord and not on the orders of the barbarian leaders."

"Then why are twelve thousand Vandali camped just across the river?" Hostilius asked.

"My guess would be they are honouring one of their gods or mayhap it's time for their annual get-together", he said with a slur that did little to complement his haughty tone. "You know, I have been told that they allow their peasants to speak in the presence of the nobles. Imagine that", he added with a guffaw.

"We must venture across the frozen river and destroy the Vandali", I said.

"What you are suggesting is contrary to the wishes of the conscript fathers", Quintillus cautioned. "Rome has long abandoned its policy of invading the lands of our peace-loving neighbours, even if they are uncouth savages. Nowadays we embrace the cultures of others and attack only those who dare breach the borders of the Empire."

"When I lived amongst the people of the eastern plains, an elder told me a tale of a bear that was hounded by a pack of wolves", I said.

"Yes, yes", Quintillus said. "It nearly slipped my mind that you are not a pureblood Roman, legate. Were it not for Gallienus, you would still be wallowing amongst the *head count*."

I ignored the fool.

"One day the wolves left the familiar open plains and sneaked into the dark forest to attack their rival", I continued. "But the bear knew the lay of the land and lured the wolves into the swamps where it killed them all."

I looked Quintillus in the eye and took a sip from my cup.

"But the bear was not content with its victory. It left the safety of the forest and ventured onto the plains in search of the den of the wolves. He surprised them and ripped open the throats of all that remained of the pack. Never again was he bothered by the vermin."

"A quaint little tale", Quintillus said, suppressed a yawn with an open palm, and started to rise. "I would not mind listening to your children's fables all night, legate, but the battle has drained me and I wish to get to bed."

Marcus met my gaze. "You are right, Lucius", he said. "We will wait for the legion to arrive. As soon as they do, we will cross the river and kill the Vandali before they grow stronger and attack us."

Quintillus slumped back onto the couch.

"This is an outrage", he slurred. "I was sent by the conscript fathers to advise you, but you have no regard for their wishes. They warned me that you would not listen, but I offered my services nonetheless - we share the same blood after all. But now I see that you allow yourself to be influenced by peasants and barbarians."

I was tired and at the end of my tether. "All I hear is the whining of a coward", I mumbled under my breath, and gained my feet.

"What did you say?" Quintillus barked.

I turned to face Marcus. "I will return at your command, lord emperor", I said, bowed, and walked into the night with Hostilius following close behind.

* * *

Diocles, Cai, Gordas, Hostilius and Adelgunde joined Segelinde and me around the dinner table later that evening.

"You need to eliminate Quintillus", Segelinde said after I had recounted the tale.

The Primus Pilus stopped chewing and reached for his cup - a clear indication that he was about to throw in his weight behind my wife's words.

"You sound like Hostilius", I said to Segelinde. "Killing cannot be the answer to every problem."

"Not every problem", the Primus Pilus said. "But most."

I noticed Gordas nod in support of Segelinde and Hostilius.

"While carry firewood, best try not put out fire", Cai said, and took a sip from his cup. "Water better than fire to put out flames."

My aide shared the Easterner's view. "Alienating Quintillus, from our perspective, seems like the right thing to do, but it is sure to make the emperor's task much more difficult", Diocles said. "Once Emperor Claudius has secured the Danubian frontier he will most probably return to Rome to garnish support for campaigns against the breakaway parts of the

Empire. If the senate is pitted against him, he will be faced with an almost impossible task."

"Mayhap we should leave this for Marcus to deal with", I sighed. "He is the emperor after all."

"Your words are wise", Segelinde said. "But wisdom and tolerance are not the right weapons to combat men who serve the darkness. Sometimes the keen edge of a blade is needed to extinguish evil."

* * *

Mid-morning the following day, Marcus and Vibius arrived at the gates of my villa amid a gentle snowfall. The emperor of Rome issued a command, and the mounted guardsmen cantered down the road, heading back to Sirmium.

"You have come", I said as I opened the gates.

"I would not miss it for the world", Marcus said.

I looked past Marcus's shoulder, as if trying to find someone. "Where is Quintillus?"

"As far as my brother is concerned, Vibius and I have ridden west to reconnoitre the movements of the Vandali. Truth is, we needed to get away from prying eyes and lying tongues that speak only the words that they think I wish to hear."

"Then you've come to the right place, lord emperor", Hostilius said. "In this villa we say it like it is. Good thing you didn't bring your brother along, besides, Domitius's woman doesn't fancy him so he'd probably wake up with a Goth dagger buried between his shoulder blades if you did."

"By the gods, tribune, it is good to be home", Marcus grinned, slapped the Primus Pilus's back, and handed his horse's reins to Felix.

The snow cleared up before midday, prompting Marcus and me to take a leisurely ride around the farm. Diocles and Cai remained at the villa, close to the braziers with their noses in scrolls, while Hostilius, Gordas and Vibius went to visit the Primus Pilus's boys who had been toiling in the hills under Pezhman's guidance.

"Hostilius wasn't jesting about Segelinde wanting to get rid of Quintillus", I said. "Kniva's murder has affected her much."

"I know", Marcus replied. "Do you remember the first time we met the siblings all those years ago when Emperor Maximinus Thrax sent us into the Goth hinterland?"

"I dwell on it often", I replied. "Which, if Diocles's scrolls are to believed, is a sign that I am getting old."

"Sometimes I think that you should have been emperor in my place, Lucius", Marcus said. "This issue with the senate and my brother consumes my thoughts. The gods know, I may be too meek to dig the Empire out of the hole it finds itself in. You, on the other hand, would not hesitate to remove those who stand in your way."

I issued a guffaw.

"Why do you laugh?" Marcus asked.

"Because, my friend, I often thank the gods that you hold the reins of the Empire", I said. "If it were me there would be too much blood. My capacity for mercy is limited - blame my upbringing if you wish. Your clemency is not a weakness, it is a strength that Rome needs in its difficult hour. Have no concern, Marcus, whenever you get to the end of your tether, I will be your sword."

Chapter 24 – Invaders

That evening we all gathered in the dining room. Around the table, three seats remained empty as a reminder of the ones we had lost along the way. As the head of the household, I gave thanks to the gods for the rebirth of the sun that once again ushered in a new year. Then I raised my cup and drank a toast to Nik, Kniva and Egnatius. "We honour our friends and family who had crossed the bridge of stars and wait for us on the other side. One day we will be reunited."

The solstice celebration was a welcome distraction. It turned out to be an enjoyable evening filled with laughter, wine and song.

For some reason or other I found that my gaze often settled on the vacant seats around the table. I could not help but ponder whether, come the next solstice, there would be more.

* * *

A watch before sunset the following day, sixty mounted praetorians trotted up to the gates of my villa to escort their emperor back to Sirmium.

"The legion will arrive on the overmorrow", Marcus said as we said our goodbyes. "If I take them across the ice and fall on the barbarians who are encamped on the northern bank of the Danube, it will cause a rift between me and the senate."

I nodded my agreement and allowed him to voice his thoughts.

"But the Vandali have tasted the spoils of Rome", he sighed. "If we do not destroy them they will bide their time and invade again as soon as the Roxolani are engaged in the north and the legions have departed."

"The only other option is to offer them peace", he continued. "But then the barbarians will think us weak and demand much gold in return. The legions would despise me for filling the pockets of the Germani with coin."

He drew a deep breath. "You see, Lucius, it is a matter of choosing between the lesser of evils."

I had given much thought to the words of my friend and believed that in this case, the logical action was not necessarily the correct action. "Mayhap there is another way", I said.

"Mayhap the Vandali will sue for peace and it will be them who pay us gold."

A frown settled on the emperor's brow and he narrowed his eyes. "Why would you think that?"

I shrugged noncommittally. "Call it a premonition", I replied.

"When?" he asked.

"In six days' time, deploy the legion in battle formation on the southern bank of the river", I said.

* * *

Hostilius, Gordas and I reined in at the crest of a hill overlooking the sprawling Roxolani winter camp. As soon as we spied horsemen galloping towards us, we dropped our open palms to our sides.

Burdukhan, the ringman of my daughter, approached at a walk, halted his mare, and inclined his head. "Lord Eochar", he said. "We have not been forewarned of your arrival."

"Greetings, Burdukhan", I said. "I see that the queen has placed great trust in you by giving you command of the tribe during her absence."

The hulking oathsworn beamed at my words. "As always, lord, you are welcome at the hearths of your mother's people", he replied.

"How goes the war in the north?" I asked.

"The tribes that mine the northern mountains descended onto the flatland in great numbers", he said. "Like so many before them they made the mistake of counting our warriors instead of counting our arrows. Messengers tell of a great battle in which Queen Aritê slaughtered thousands of the hillmen. A train of wagons with slaves and plunder is on its way to our camp, but the queen is pushing north to serve her wrath upon the dirt eaters."

For a moment I pitied the hillmen. The wrath of my daughter could be a terrible thing.

"I share in your joy", I said. "Like you, the blood of the horse lords of the Roxolani courses through my veins."

"Come, Lord Eochar", he said, and acknowledged Hostilius and Gordas with a nod. "You and your oathsworn will warm yourselves beside my hearth. Let us share a cup and the bounty of the land."

* * *

We sat cross-legged on soft furs around a wood fire while outside the hide-covered felt, a howling gale ripped at the braided ropes. Juices dripped from the meat onto the embers, filling the inside of Burdukhan's tent with the aroma of woodsmoke and cooked mutton.

Gordas leaned forward, twisted a joint from the carcass, and handed it to our host.

Burdukhan tore at the pink flesh with his teeth and washed it down with a swig of fermented milk before indicating that we should partake in the feast. "All know that you walk in the shadow of Arash, lord", the big man said. "Are you in need of the bows and spears of the Roxolani?"

"You know me well", I replied.

Hostilius grunted his agreement and dipped a chunk of flatbread into the clay bowl that collected most of the dripping fat and juices. He wrapped the moist unleavened bread around a piece of soft cheese, popped it into his mouth, and took a gulp of mead.

"I need three thousand boys or maidens who are strong enough to draw a warrior's bow, but too young to go to war", I said.

A frown creased the champion's brow.

"I also require the services of two thousand of your warriors who are too old to ride into battle", I said.

His frown deepened. "I do not understand, lord."

I held out my cup for a refill and explained it to him.

* * *

Three days later, half a watch before first light, Hostilius, Gordas and I walked our horses across the frozen white expanse of the Danube. The blizzard of the previous days had calmed, but in its wake came light but seemingly interminable snow.

"I hate riding across the frozen river", Hostilius whispered. "The gods only know which of Hades's creatures lurk in the dark waters beneath the ice."

He had hardly finished speaking when there was a sharp crack somewhere between us and the far bank. The noise was followed by a slight tremor which made us stop in our tracks.

Kasirga issued a nicker and his ears pricked up. Moments later, squinting through the snow into the pre-dawn light, we spied dark shapes behind us.

"Wolves", Hostilius whispered, and made to spur his gelding. "Come, let's get to the far bank before more of these vermin get their courage up."

"Beware, Roman", Gordas hissed, and grabbed the Primus Pilus's arm.

The Hun reached for his wolf foot charm. "My grandfather warned me about apparitions that appear in the midst of a winter storm during the time of the solstice. They are the wolves of Karachun, the dark lord of blizzards. He has sent them to herd us to our doom." He turned his mare towards the dark shapes who retreated before us.

With our hands clasped around our amulets we followed Gordas, who led us east, parallel to the far bank. As he turned the head of his horse towards the southern bank, what appeared to be a horse and rider, galloped silently across the snow at the edge of our field of vision.

"Marzanna", Gordas said as a shiver made its way down my spine. "The woman of Karachun, the one who brings death."

Only when Kasirga powered up the incline of the far bank did I let go of my amulet. The snow stopped falling and the first golden rays of the rising sun lit the eastern horizon. We reined in on the solid ground and gazed across the mile-wide Danube. "Look", Gordas said, and pointed at a crevasse in the ice, nearly four paces wide and twenty across.

"It seems that your grandfather was right", I said.

"At least we managed to foil Marzanna and her man", Hostilius said, his hand still under his fur cloak.

Gordas issued a grunt of agreement. Unbeknown to the Hun, the bringers of death and calamity had already spawned their evil.

Chapter 25 – Vandali

We found the *IV Flavia Felix* drawn up for battle. The legion was deployed in open formation on a snow-covered fallow field overlooking the Danube. The legionary cavalry on the flanks had been bolstered by the five hundred available Illyrians as well as the mounted praetorians who protected the emperor.

At the head of the army, I recognised the standard of Emperor Claudius Gothicus, conqueror of the Goths and destroyer of the Alemanni. Amongst his retinue I spied Vibius, Diocles and Quintillus. Across the flat expanse of the frozen river, thousands of fur-clad tribesmen darkened the south-facing slope of the gentle incline. I recognised the blue banners of the Vandali, the blackened bear skulls of the Lugii and the ochre furs of the Buri.

The praetorians parted as we approached, allowing us access to their commander.

I inclined my head to Marcus. "Lord Emperor", I said.

"I assume that you are not here to dissuade my brother from the foolish notion of attacking the barbarians", Quintillus said, and reached for his wineskin. He offered it to the emperor first, who accepted it with a nod.

"What do you suggest, Legate Domitius?" Marcus asked, took a swig, and offered it to me.

I declined with a raised palm. "Let us ride out to the Vandali", I said. "If things go awry, I wish to have my wits about me."

I noticed that, despite the chill, Quintillus was sweating profusely. At the time I believed it to be a sign of fear.

"Come, we will parley", Marcus said, and indicated for his brother to join us.

Marcus, Quintillus, Hostilius, Gordas, Vibius, Diocles and I guided our mounts onto the ice. Close to the middle of the river we reined in.

Soon an equal number of mounted tribesmen parted from the barbarian host and made their way towards us. They halted ten paces away.

Wisimar, the war chief of the Vandali, wore the blue wool *braccae* that identified him as a noble of his tribe. Because of the bitter cold, a knee-length cloak of wolfskin was draped around his broad shoulders. Underneath the furs his burnished scale armour sparkled like the sun.

"Lord Wisimar", Marcus said, and gestured at the thousands of chanting warriors. "Why do you bring your army to the territory of Rome?"

The war leader indicated the southern bank of the Danube. "Rome took those lands from the Amantini and the Scordisci by the power of the sword", Wisimar said. "Today is our turn to take it from you."

"May I make a suggestion?" I said, my words drawing the Vandali king's gaze.

"You! You are the half-breed who sired the bitch-queen of the Scythians", Wisimar spat. "She is driving my people from their rightful lands. Today you will not be rescued by her horsemen, they are campaigning against my allies far to the north."

"How much?" Quintillus asked, eager to bribe the savages in order to avoid a battle.

A smile of triumph broke Wisimar's bearded face. "I thought that you would rather offer me tribute than face our spears", he said. "Three talents of gold will suffice."

"If coin is going to change hands, may I be so bold to suggest that it should be four talents", I said. "The only difference being that the Vandali pay us instead?"

A frown of confusion furrowed Wisimar's brow. Quintillus stared at me, his expression incredulous.

Before the war chief could reply, I raised an arm. Silhouetted against the rising sun, thousands of Roxolani horsemen crested the hill behind the Vandali. The appearance of the Scythians meant that the invaders were surrounded, trapped between the barbarian riders and the legion.

"With your permission, lord", I said to Wisimar, "I would like to introduce a friend."

The Vandali war chief realised the precariousness of their situation and acquiesced with a nod. On his order, his standard bearer issued a note on the ram's horn.

On the crest of the hill, a lone rider broke away from the ranks. He approached slowly and purposefully, guiding his stallion through the sea of Germani who had parted on the command of their leader.

Five hundred heartbeats later, Burdukhan reined in beside me, the severed heads of three Vandali scouts dangling from his saddle. His scale armour was polished to a brilliant shine and his horse painted for war. "Lord Eochar", he said. "Our mounts are rested, our bows strung and our shafts smeared with the venom of adders. What do you command?"

"You are a sorcerer, half-breed", Wisimar spat in frustration, his complexion as red as a beet.

"On second thought, the price for your lives has gone up to five talents", I said to Wisimar. "Choose."

* * *

The sun was high in the sky when the last stragglers of the barbarian mob crested the rise and disappeared into the hinterland. Earlier, Wisimar had handed over their plunder while Marcus had taken the sons of their nobles as hostages to ensure that the balance would be settled in good time.

I gestured to the wagons filled with loot. "That is the Roxolani's share", I said to Burdukhan. "Give my regards to the queen."

"I will do as you command, lord", he said. "Queen Aritê will be pleased."

While the legion struck camp and the Roxolani rode north, we rested in the emperor's spacious tent, waiting for the Illyrians and mounted praetorians to escort us back to Sirmium. Quintillus appeared decidedly nervous, continually fiddling with the hem of his senatorial toga. "I believe that by your actions you have shown that you are willing to accommodate the will of the senate, lord emperor", he said to Marcus. "I wish to return to Rome to report my findings to the conscript fathers in person."

"Surely you will first travel to Sirmium so that I am able to give you a proper send-off", the emperor said, his tone suggesting the opposite. "Besides, the passes are closed."

"I will travel to Salona", Quintillus revealed. "There, a galley is waiting to take me to Rome."

"If I didn't know better", Vibius whispered, "I'd think that he has set his travel arrangements well in advance."

"I won't be surprised if the senate has galleys dedicated for their exclusive use in all the major ports", I mused.

Vibius shrugged and passed me a cup.

The emperor stole me a glance of appreciation before continuing his conversation. "I will miss your counsel dearly, brother", he said. "For now I will remain on the frontier, but your rightful place is in the capital, aiding the senate in their tireless work."

Hostilius wore an expression of disgust as he leaned in closer. "If the emperor had asked me for advice, I'd tell him to get Gordas to follow Quintillus to Salona and slit the bastard's throat while he's sleeping", the Primus Pilus whispered. "Now that's good advice - not the drivel escaping from that idiot's mouth."

"Although it is a tempting thought, it won't be necessary", I said. "I doubt whether we will see him again soon. He will sit in the benches in the senate house and boast about how he had crushed the Vandali while he swallows down lark tongues with great gulps of falernian."

"Talking about falernian", Hostilius said. "I assume that tonight we will be celebrating our victory. I'm actually looking forward to a get-together for a change, instead of dreading to be in the same room as that fool Quintillus."

* * *

"Where is Marcus?" I asked my aide once I had taken a seat on a couch within the private dining room of the imperial palace.

"He will probably join us soon", Diocles replied while he filled my cup. "I last saw him scrutinizing the report that I compiled of the day's happenings."

"Now that the Vandali have been put in their place we can spend time at home until the campaigning season kicks off in the spring", Hostilius said, and lay back against the soft cushions. "Make no mistake, I enjoy the life of a soldier, but every man wants the opportunity to sit beside his own hearth once in a while."

We all raised our cups to drink to Hostilius's words.

There was a knock at the door, and the imperial chamberlain shuffled in. "Legate", he said, addressing me. "Our Lord Caesar is slightly under the weather this evening. He is exhausted and has retired early. He asks that you do not depart on the morrow before he has had an opportunity to speak with you."

"You see, we aren't the only ones who's tired from kicking barbarian arse", Hostilius said, raising his cup for another toast as soon as the chamberlain had gone. "The emperor's done more in a year that Gallienus had in twenty. He deserves a rest."

Again we raised our cups, this time drinking to the health of Emperor Claudius Gothicus.

Chapter 26 – Malady

"What do you mean the emperor is still sleeping?" Hostilius asked and walked towards the chamberlain in the same menacing manner I had seen him stroll into battle. Few men would not have been intimidated by the scowling, bull-like Primus Pilus.

The chamberlain was not one of them.

The terrified functionary opened his palms and extended his arms in front of him in what I believed to be a placating gesture. "Please, tribune", he said. "Please. The lord emperor is very tired."

"Bollocks", Hostilius said. "He's a soldier. I've never seen him sleep past sunrise and he's sure as hades not going to start now."

The chamberlain looked to me for assistance. "I have witnessed Tribune Proculus rip men apart with his bare hands", I said. "I suggest you step aside."

Wisely, the man complied.

We found Marcus still in bed, propped up against soft cushions and covered with furs. Beside him sat two men whom I recognised as the imperial physicians. Our friend's complexion was pale, his eyes tired.

"The emperor has contracted a fever and needs to rest", the physician nearest to us scolded.

Marcus weakly gestured to the men flanking his bed. "They do not wish to tell me to my face, but I suspect that I have the plague", he croaked. "Am I right?"

The same man who chastised us started to protest, but Marcus silenced him with a flick of a wrist. "Answer me", he demanded, the authority thick in his voice.

The doctor bowed his head. "It is as you say, Lord Emperor."

"Leave us", Marcus commanded.

While the physicians scampered from the room, I glanced over my shoulder and my eyes locked with Gordas's. I needed no words.

"I will fetch the Easterner", he said. Heartbeats later, I heard his mare's hooves pound the cobbles of the courtyard.

I kneeled beside the bed and gestured for Hostilius, Vibius and Diocles to keep their distance. "Cai believes that one cannot be struck down by this illness twice, and I have been afflicted with it before", I said. "Open the shutters so that the bad air may escape."

* * *

"Not plague", Cai said, and softly closed the ornate doors of the emperor's bedroom behind him.

I made to enter to share the good news with my friend, but Cai stopped me with a palm against the chest. "I give him potion. He sleep. Come Lucius of Da Qin, we talk", he said, and led the way to the study where Hostilius, Gordas, Vibius and Diocles were waiting.

"It's not the plague", I said, unable to contain myself from sharing the good tidings with my friends.

"Thank the gods", Hostilius said.

Cai raised a palm. "It poison."

The Easterner's words stunned us into silence.

"Toadstool of Hades", Cai explained.

"Marcus knows that he has enemies on both sides of the Danube", Vibius said. "He never eats or drinks anything unless it has been tasted."

"None of his tasters are even remotely ill", Hostilius said. "I've checked already."

"Toadstool of Hades very, very bad poison", Cai continued. "No antidote."

"Are you saying that he will die?" Diocles asked.

"Gods decide on who die, who live", Cai replied. "I say it very bad poison."

An unexpected dizziness took hold of me and I slumped down onto the nearest couch. It felt as if what we had toiled for all our lives was coming apart like a badly-stitched cloak. I buried my face in my palms and prayed to Arash.

"If he's been poisoned, we have to find out who did it", Hostilius said as he gained his feet. "Stop feeling sorry for yourself, Domitius. Come, we need to run an errand." He turned to Gordas and Vibius. "You too."

Diocles reached for his cloak, but Hostilius stopped him with a glare. "Better stay here, Greek", he said. "Scrolls won't help you where were we're going."

"I'm not taking a scroll", my aide replied, and strapped on his dagger.

* * *

Hostilius led us from the palace complex across the forum. In silence we continued along the main thoroughfare flanked by the watercourse, and turned right just after we passed through the main gates. Like most Roman cities, Sirmium had long past outgrown its walls. Outside the fortifications, on the wet, swampy ground bordering the river, a second, informal town had taken root.

"Where are we going?" Diocles asked as we entered the slum.

"Long ago, I served with a man from Cyrenaica", the Primus Pilus said. "I expelled him from the legion."

Hostilius did not elaborate, and Diocles managed to keep his curiosity in check.

The wooden structures were built and occupied by creatures who could not afford to reside inside the stone walls, or by those whose activities necessitated the option of a quick escape. We made our way along crooked, mud-slick paths that reeked of detritus. Through the veil of charcoal smoke, we spied emaciated men, women and children watching us from inside makeshift huts and lean-tos where they huddled around cooking fires, sipping on sour wine or thin gruel.

"Here we are", Hostilius said, coming to a halt in front of a shack that seemed sturdier than most. He banged on the door with a balled fist. The entire building shuddered under the onslaught. For a moment I feared that the structure would collapse, but it held firm.

The Primus Pilus stopped knocking and stepped back when a wet cough emanated from the other side of the sagging, leather-hinged door. Slowly it slid open, the bottom edge of the wood scraping away a pile of muddy filth. A heartbeat later, a swarthy man with lank black hair stepped from the gloom into the light.

"Garaman", Hostilius said, his tone indifferent.

"Centurion", the man replied and extended his arm, which the Primus Pilus gripped in the way of the warrior.

"I wish to find the rootcutters", he said. "Know you of any who have come to Sirmium?"

"The travelling people keep to themselves", he said, his accent heavy. "The Marsi keep no schedule."

Hostilius took a step closer to Garaman until a handspan separated their faces. "You can tell me now, or you can tell me while you're hanging from a cross on the hill over yonder", he growled, and gestured to the high ground where criminals were executed.

For long, the man from Cyrenaica considered Hostilius's words. Then his shoulders slumped. "A band of Marsi came through here a week ago", he said. "They left yesterday."

"Where do I search?" Hostilius asked.

"You will find them on the road to Cibalae", Garaman replied.

* * *

Just before the start of the second watch of the morning, we exited through the gates of Sirmium. We cantered along the open ground bordering the road so that the pounding of hooves would not alert travellers.

"Why did you dismiss that man from the legion?" Diocles asked.

"He ran a business while he was enrolled", Hostilius stated.

"Strictly speaking, it is prohibited", Diocles confirmed, "but we both know that, er…, commercial activities are tolerated if they do not interfere with the workings of the legion."

"He kept a pouch of vipers underneath his bed to sell to druggists", Hostilius said.

"Oh", my aide replied.

Ten miles west of the city we came upon a small convoy of mule carts. At least a dozen women and children sat in the back of the wagons, while roughly the same number of men trudged alongside. They veered off the road into the shrubbery as soon as they noticed us, but it helped them naught.

We thundered off the road, intercepting them where the cart track crossed a stream and ascended into forested hills.

"We need to speak with you", Hostilius told the oldster who held the reins of the draught animals. "We are on the emperor's business."

Slowly the men on foot positioned themselves on both sides of the wagon, their sword hands hidden underneath their ragged cloaks.

The Marsi resided in the mountainous high country not far from the Eternal City. They were an ancient people who had marginalised themselves by holding on to their customs. They still served the old gods and clung to their archaic practices of snake charming and dark magic. The travelling people, as some called them, earned their coin by selling roots and potions and robbing the odd traveller they chanced upon.

They were also known as tough men who knew how to handle weapons. I did not fail to notice the scars criss-crossing the forearms and faces of the men who flanked the oldster.

The Marsi driving the cart looked us over, no doubt sizing us up. He seemed unconcerned that we were the emperor's men.

"Don't care if you are on the business of Jupiter himself", he smirked, and spat out a glob of phlegm. "Get out of my way. We still need to harvest the forest, and", he said, and used a holed boot to lift the lid of the wooden box his feet rested upon, "trap rats to feed them snakes."

Through the crack I spied a writhing mass of adders.

"To whom did you sell poison?" I asked, and clasped a fist around the hilt of my blade. "Give me a name or description and you may go your own way, charmer."

"Like I said", he replied, and reached inside the container, presumably to take hold of a viper. "It's none of your bus…"

I was in no mood to suffer fools.

"Aargh!" he screamed as his severed fingers dropped into the box of adders. The keen edge of my blade came to rest against his jugular. Roused by the smell of blood, the creatures slithered vigorously, eager to devour the unexpected windfall.

The man to the right of the oldster was first to draw his sword, or at least first to try.

The bronze butt of Hostilius's boar spear slammed into the side of the Marsi's head before his blade was out of the scabbard, and he collapsed where he stood.

The man beside him let out a roar and charged at me, a dagger in his fist.

Gordas's braided lasso plucked him from his feet. He lay writhing in the shallow water, both hands clamped around the rope depriving him of breath.

"Stop in the name of Angitia!" the oldster boomed.

His men's hands dropped to their sides.

"He came in the night, wearing a *sagum*", the old Marsi said whilst carefully wrapping his bleeding appendages with a dirty strip of linen. "He gave me no name and I did not ask - our business is… discreetness."

"You have to do better than that", I said, drawing a drop of blood with my blade.

"His... his breath stank of wine", the Marsi stammered. "Although he spoke like them senators in Rome, he slurred his words like a drunk in a tavern. And he had six ruffians with him, all hard-looking men."

"How many senators in Sirmium slur after their second cup?" Hostilius asked through clenched teeth. "And how many of those have six tame guards?"

"What did you sell him?" I asked the Marsi.

"Toadstools of Hades", the oldster replied.

Chapter 27 – Slur (February 270 AD)

"Quintillus is responsible", I concluded after recounting the happenings earlier in the day.

"I doubt that he had the opportunity", Marcus replied, wincing as a cramp racked his body. "I never accepted food or wine from his hand."

"Never?" I asked.

Marcus thought on my words, then clenched his teeth while he waited for the spasms to dissipate. "Once", he acknowledged with a nod. "Just before we spoke with the Vandali war leader."

He gestured for me to help him take a swallow of the poppy potion that Cai had concocted. I held the cup to his lips. He took a sip, then slumped back against the cushions to allow the remedy to do its work.

When the drug had taken effect he sat up again.

"I suspect that I am dying, Lucius", he said.

"Marcus, I..", but I got no further.

"Lucius", he said, and smiled a wan smile. "I know when you are about to tell a lie."

I pursed my lips and nodded. "Cai says that it is in the hands of the gods."

"Do you remember when our paths crossed the first time?" he asked, changing the subject.

"How can I forget", I said.

"If it were not for you, I would have died that day", he said. "Apart from your friendship, you have given me more than thirty years... and it has been good."

Marcus turned his face towards the frescoed wall. I sat beside his bed in silence, allowing him time to gather himself.

"Not long ago you told me that I was the better man to sit on the Roman throne", he said. "You were wrong."

I made to protest, but he silenced me by lifting a palm.

"You said that unlike me, you were too uncompromising, too prone to violence", he said.

"I still think so", I replied.

Marcus reached out and gripped my forearm, his palm cold and sweat-slick. "Had we lived a thousand lifetimes, you would have been right in all but one. But the gods have chosen to place us on this earth at a time like no other. From inside and out, the Empire is besieged by black-hearted men who care little for honour and even less for the lives of others. I have been blind not to see it, but now it is clear - this, Lucius, is your time, not mine. It is time for an emperor who has little capacity for mercy, a warrior who will rid the world of the decay that has somehow managed to take hold."

I did not answer, just sat in silence beside my dying friend.

Once again, he asked for a sip of potion and waited for the pain to ease. Then his eyes closed and he drifted off to sleep.

* * *

Most days I feared that my friend would not see the next sunrise, while at other times I imagined that he had turned the corner and would recover. He banned the imperial physicians from his chambers, relying on Cai to ease his suffering. For a reason that only became clear later, Marcus did not wish to let outsiders know that he had been poisoned. Apart from us, his inner circle, and Quintillus, of course, all believed that the emperor was afflicted with the plague.

Early in the morning of the seventeenth day after he fell ill, Vibius, who had been with Marcus, woke me up. "He asks for you."

I wrapped a fur around my shoulders and we made our way to the imperial bed chamber. I nodded to the praetorians flanking the entrance, closed the door behind us, and kneeled beside the bed while Vibius sat at the base.

"I need you to give me an oath, Lucius", Marcus said, his voice weak. "Vibius and the gods are my witnesses."

"Anything", I replied.

"Swear that you will take up the purple when I am gone", he whispered. "And give me your word that you will not harm Quintillus."

I hesitated.

"Be quick, before it is too late", he jested, his jaw tightening as he willed away another spasm.

"I give my oath on my honour as a Scythian", I replied, which made him grin.

"I see that you still believe that the oath of a Scythian is superior to that of a Roman's", Marcus said.

"I do", I replied.

Neither Marcus nor Vibius understood why I had used the words I had.

* * *

Later that same day, just before sunset, Emperor Marcus Aurelius Claudius crossed the river. The tears we shed were not only for the loss of a friend, but we cried on behalf of the Empire who had lost one of their greatest emperors.

In Marcus's short rein he had destroyed the fearsome Goths, crushed the Alemanni and cowered the Vandali into submission. Like Hostilius said, he had achieved more in a year than ten emperors had in the last hundred.

Throughout the palace we could hear the wails of mourners as we surrendered Marcus's body to the *libitinarii*, who, like carrion birds watching a wounded stag, had been waiting for the inevitable. I walked back to my room along the cold marble halls in a trance-like state, and it felt as if I was in the midst of a dark dream that I would soon wake up from to discover that all was still well.

Exhausted by the hours spent in vigil, I lay down and was asleep even before I could cover myself with a fur.

* * *

I woke at the grey hour of the wolf, shivering from the terrible cold, still in the same posture as when I had fallen asleep. The door slowly squeaked open and my hand found the hilt of my dagger.

Hostilius's head appeared in the crack. "Come in", I said.

While I splashed my face with water from the enamelled basin beside the bed, the Primus Pilus poured wine.

"You must take up the purple, Domitius", he said as he handed me a cup.

"Marcus's body is barely cold", I replied. "Let us first mourn our friend's passing. When we have sent his shade across the bridge of stars, we will discuss the way forward."

"Have it your way", Hostilius said.

For nine days we observed the last rites of the great man. On the morning of the tenth day after the emperor's passing,

Hostilius, Vibius and I, who were closest to him in life, led the funerary procession through the streets of Sirmium, heading to the forum packed with thousands of mourners. His body, laid out on a purple couch decorated with ivory, was placed on top of a latticework of five thousand Roman spears. The day before, the men of the *IV Flavia Felix* had honoured their emperor by each laying a *pilum* for the fire that would transport his shade to Elysium.

After the interminable eulogies, the high priest of Ceres sacrificed a sow to ensure that the goddess, who was the doorwarden of Hades's gates, would assist the emperor's shade to pass to the afterlife.

When all was done, I took up the torch, lit from the sacred fire in the temple of Vesta, and thrust it into the pyre of spear hafts that had been wetted with oil.

The flames burned bright and hot, forcing me to take a few steps back.

Inside my chest an even hotter fire had been lit - the all-consuming fire of revenge.

* * *

That evening we went home to celebrate Marcus's life. To ease his passing, we sat around a fire blazing in the hearth, drank fine wine, and shared tales of our friend's exploits.

I recounted the story of how Marcus and I had met and how he had fallen off his horse. Segelinde told of how two young Romans had arrived before the gates of a Goth town many years before. Gordas reminded us of the time we spent campaigning in the lands of Sasania. With his stories of set battles, Hostilius took us back to the time when Marcus, then stationed in Germania Superior, had led Gallienus's armies against the Franks.

* * *

I was up early the following morning. I added kindling to the hearth fire, and once I had flames I heated some milk and added a palmful of coarse salt.

There was no stirring in their rooms, so I assumed that Hostilius and Gordas were still caught up in Bacchus's embrace.

I sat down on a couch and sipped on the salty brew while I organised my thoughts.

Vibius walked in and took a place opposite me.

I offered him a cup and he accepted with a grateful nod.

"What do we do now?" he asked.

There was no doubt in my mind what needed to be done. "Help me with my armour", I said, causing my friend to raise an eyebrow.

"I will ride west to find Quintillus", I said while Vibius tightened the buckles at the back of my scale vest. For a moment he paused, but then continued without a word.

"You swore an oath to a dying man", my friend eventually said after thirty heartbeats had passed.

"I gave him my word as a Scythian", I said. "Scythians believe that one is freed from one's oaths by death."

Vibius did not reply at first but focused on fitting my greaves. When he was done, he raised himself and looked me square in the eye. "You lied to him, Lucius."

I lowered my eyes in shame. "I did", I confessed. "While I said the words to placate Marcus I made another oath of my own to Arash."

"I thought you said that all oaths are nullified by death?" he replied.

"All but one", I said. "An oath of vengeance to the lord of blood is binding and stronger than death itself."

Vibius shook his head and turned towards the door.

"Are you turning your back on me?" I said, my tone more tired than judgemental.

"No", he replied. "I'll be back once I've strapped on my sword belt."

* * *

Hostilius had read me like a scroll. Vibius and I found him and Gordas in the stables, kitted out in full armour and their weapons strapped to their saddles. Cai was there as well, dressed in one of his loose-fitting robes.

"Have you seen Diocles?" I asked no one in particular, acting as if we had planned the trip the night before.

"He's gone ahead to Sirmium", the Primus Pilus replied while checking his horse's tack.

In silence, we trotted along the road that led to the city.

Outside the gates of Sirmium, Diocles waited at the head of five hundred Illyrians and the same number of mounted praetorians. They were formed up in a column, complete with their packhorses and baggage.

I gave Hostilius a sidelong glance.

"We know you well enough by now, Domitius", the Primus Pilus muttered, keeping his eyes to the front.

We fell in beside Diocles, and on my command the standard bearer signalled the advance.

Chapter 28 – Aquileia (April 270 AD)

I barely noticed Hortensius lift a little finger. The servants who were watching their master like hawks sprang into action, clearing the empty dishes in a matter of heartbeats. The last to disappear from the dining room discreetly and silently closed the double doors.

"Is it not to your liking?" our host asked as he removed a stewed mushroom from the yet untouched dish in order to sample it. "I collect them myself, you know."

"They look delicious", I replied earnestly. "It's just that, er…, we have much on our minds."

"Of course", Hortensius said. "Forgive me my insensitivity, Legate Domitius. Emperor Claudius Gothicus was a great man indeed."

I nodded and took a swallow of sweet white wine.

"Word on the street is that the senate plans to elevate Quintillus to the purple", the innkeeper said, his voice low. "Only yesterday a travelling merchant told me that the legions based in Raetia and Noricum have been ordered to rendezvous with the new emperor at Aquileia. They are crossing the passes as we speak."

"Obviously to enforce Quintillus's succession", Diocles remarked.

"Are you and your entourage also on your way to Aquileia to give your oath to the new emperor?" Hortensius asked.

"We plan to give the new emperor that which he deserves", I confirmed.

* * *

Early morning four days later, we reined in halfway down the steep decline of the Pear Tree Pass. The track followed the contours of the slope, winding its way down a cliffside path that cut through an ancient forest of pine and spruce.

"A Roman legion's been through here. Maybe even two", Hostilius said, his eyes fixed on the churned-up sludge of mud and snow. In the centre of the track, deep indentations were visible, imprinted by the heavy ox wagons of the Roman army.

"We've got a thousand riders", Hostilius continued, "the best that the Empire is able to muster. With you leading them, I would take on a legion. But two legions?"

I had been praying non-stop to Arash to deliver us from the predicament of my own making, but the god gave me no guidance. I tried to appear confident, and shrugged at the Primus Pilus's concerns. "Let us cross that bridge when we get there, eh?"

Early afternoon that same day, we approached the Roman bridge spanning the Aesontius. While we watered the horses, Hostilius passed me the reins of his gelding. "It's the last proper river before we get to Aquileia", he said, narrowing his eyes. "Since you haven't got a plan, I might as well go and offer sacrifices, just in case the next river we'll be crossing turns out to be the Styx."

The Primus Pilus stomped off to where a peasant was selling wine and barley cakes near a small altar dedicated to the god of the river. I saw him exchange words with the peddler before pouring a libation of wine onto the stone and casting the cakes into the thundering water. When he returned, we were already mounted and ready to ride. I was so preoccupied with concerns regarding our immediate future that I failed to give heed to the frown on Hostilius's brow.

The road continued along the western bank of the river, leading us through blossoming apple and pear orchards. We passed low stone walls enclosing vineyards where the first smattering of green already decorated vines that would soon be heavy with grapes. On the flat ground bordering the river, peasant farmers were labouring behind ox-drawn ploughs to prepare the recently flooded fields for wheat, oats and barley.

Not long after, we rounded the high ground on our left and descended onto the plain north of Aquileia. It was hard to miss the two Roman legions that were deployed in open formation, ready to give battle. At the centre of the army, a contingent of praetorians clustered around a rider adorned with a purple cloak and mounted on a pure white stallion.

I reined in, and on my command the standard bearer relayed my orders. With an ease that comes with countless watches of practise, the thousand horsemen deployed on the plain, matching the frontage of the legions.

"Do we attack?" Gordas asked, and put an arrow to the string of his horn bow.

"I've come for revenge", I said, "not to spill the blood of fellow Romans."

"What do we do then?" Vibius asked.

Arash was still silent and I had no plan to speak of. I wondered why the lord of blood had brought me this far only to abandon me at the last moment. But the gods can be fickle.

"I have an idea", Hostilius blurted out. "When I sacrificed at the Aesontius, Mars spoke to me."

I trusted the Primus Pilus implicitly. "Then let us abide the god of war", I said, only too glad to have received divine guidance.

"I hate this", the Primus Pilus mumbled, walked his horse off the cobbles, leaned from the saddle, and broke a leafy green branch from an olive tree. "It'll be you and me, Domitius", he said.

Hostilius and I walked our horses towards where the standards and banners of Quintillus's legions flapped in the breeze. We halted halfway between the armies, about three hundred paces from the front ranks of the legions.

The new emperor must have been tempted to give the command for the artillery to wipe us from the field. But he was astute enough to know that then he would be viewed as a tyrant rather than a magnanimous emperor who ruled with the support of the conscript fathers.

Quintillus's contingent separated from the ranks, and it was immediately clear that he was not taking any unnecessary chances. He was surrounded by six mounted praetorians, his most loyal men. In addition, two hard-looking, greying warriors accompanied him. Judging by their uniforms, they were the head centurions of the legions. There were no tribunes in his retinue as he had without doubt already demoted the competent plebeian officers back to the *head count* where they belonged.

"Tell me what to do", I said to Hostilius, my eyes never leaving the approaching men.

"Get him and his praetorians aside, then kill them all", the Primus Pilus suggested.

I shot Hostilius a look. "Is that your plan?" I asked. "I have to kill seven and you get to deal with two?"

He used his chin to indicate the deep ranks of legionaries just three hundred paces distant. "You got it all wrong, Domitius", he said. "I'll be taking care of twelve thousand men."

"How?" I asked.

"The primus pilus on the left is Barbius Montanus", he said, "and the other one is Cocceius Florianus. Both hard bastards."

"They look familiar", I said.

"They should", Hostilius said. "You saved them and their cohorts from certain death in that final charge when you broke the back of Tharuarus's Goths. I shared a cup with them in the *popina* in Naissus - they think you a god, Domitius."

"If you say so", I said, just as the imperial entourage reined in ten paces away. I recognised the praetorians as the same men who, during Quintillus's time in Sirmium, had followed him around like tame hounds clustering around their master. I had no doubt that they had been complicit in his plans.

"I see that you come into my presence with a sword at your hip", the brand-new emperor sneered. He wore no sword, but he made no mention of his brutes who were armed to the teeth.

"It is the barbarian way", I replied.

"It figures", he said. "Have you come to give me your oath, legate, or to fight?" he added with the supreme confidence of a man with twelve thousand Roman legionaries at his back.

Quintillus was unaware of the fact that we knew that Marcus had been poisoned. Even if we had arrived at that conclusion, he would still have thought it highly unlikely that we had uncovered his guilt. I thought it best to bring his treachery into the open.

"We need to speak with you about a band of Marsi rootcutters, Lord Emperor", I said.

The colour drained from Quintillus's face and I could see his mind working behind his beady eyes. "Give us privacy", he instructed the first centurions, who bowed and put themselves out of earshot.

I turned to Hostilius and barked at him as if he was an underling. "You heard the emperor, did you not?"

"Legate", he said, "I understand and I will obey", and strolled off to join the two centurions.

Quintillus raised an eyebrow. "Pity you have no breeding", he said. "You could have served me well."

From the corner of my eye I noticed Hostilius talking to the two men who, for all practical purposes, commanded the loyalty of the twelve thousand men behind them. I knew that he needed time.

"Was murdering your brother your own idea?" I asked. "Or did you act on the instructions of your masters in the senate?"

The emperor's face went from corpse-pale to bright red in a heartbeat. "I am the Roman emperor, peasant", he boomed. "No one tells me what to do."

"So it was you?" I replied.

"Just like Gallienus, Marcus flaunted the traditions of Rome by ignoring the wishes of the senate. If I didn't do it", he said, "someone else would have."

I had often heard criminals use the same words as justification for their actions. Quintillus might have been the emperor, but in my eyes he was nothing better than a murderer. "I condemn you to death", I said. "You and your accomplices."

"It is you who will die today, peasant", Quintillus said. "It is too late even for the gods to save you."

The man beside Quintillus issued a sycophantic snort.

For countless hours I had practised to draw my sword with the swiftness of a striking adder. My blade slid out of the scabbard on my left hip, flashed, and the guard's snort morphed into a gurgle as he clutched at his severed windpipe, bloody froth pouring through his fingers.

Using my wrist, I reversed the direction of the sword and flicked the honed edge across the throat of the man next to the gurgler before his own weapon was halfway out of its sheath.

The emperor was no soldier. His first reaction was not to stand and fight, but to flee, and he jerked his horse's head to the right.

Kasirga, who had sensed my mood, was as taut as a horn bow under full draw. My heels touched his sides, and the enormous stallion shot forward. His thick chest struck Quintillus's horse square on its shoulder, halfway through the turn - a massive hit that made the white horse stumble into the horses of the praetorians. The emperor went down with his mount, taking two of his bodyguards with him.

A third guard, a tall, muscular warrior with the features of a Thracian, was almost as quick as I was. But not quite. I blocked his backhanded swipe, and before he could bring his shield to bear, the spike of my battle-axe slammed into his cavalry helmet and split his skull.

I exchanged three, maybe four blows with the last man still mounted, but my Seric blade was crafted from sky-iron and his sword fractured as he tried to block a strike. His eyes were locked on the stump of his weapon as my iron split the rings of his mail and pierced his heart.

I twisted in the saddle to deal with the two guards who had earlier fallen with the emperor. Too late I saw that one man had regained his feet, his spear drawn back and his weight already transferred to his front foot. But a thick boar spear whooshed in from outside my range of vision, skewering the man like a spit-ready sheep.

The last guard was still rising on unsteady legs when Florianus ran him through with a textbook thrust from his gladius.

Hostilius crouched down and picked up the emperor's cloak that had fallen during the fight. The Primus Pilus dusted it off and approached in a manner that hinted that he wished to drape it around my shoulders.

I pointed at Quintillus whose eyes were flickering open after being stunned by the fall. "I cannot take up the purple while the emperor still lives", I said.

The Primus Pilus pointed with his gladius at Quintillus. "Kill him", he said.

Montanus, who was standing close by, shrugged noncommittally. He moved two steps closer, lifted Quintillus's head by his hair and unceremoniously drew his blade across the emperor's neck. "I've been wanting to do that for a week now", he said, and spat onto the dirt.

"Well then, Domitius", Hostilius said, a triumphant grin splitting his scarred face, "let's get it done before you change your mind again."

Chapter 29 – Emperor

That evening the Illyrians and legionaries did not spill one another's blood, but got drunk together in the taverns of Aquileia. While they spent the customary coin that they were given to smooth over the ascension of a new emperor on wine and whores, they gossiped about the events that had unfolded on the battlefield.

Apart from myself, only Hostilius, Montanus and Florianus had witnessed the demise of Quintillus. For that reason, I suspected that they were the ones who spread the rumours.

In one recounted eyewitness version, Quintillus had a fallout with his guards. Hostilius, the two centurions and I bravely defended the emperor, but he fell to the blades of his disgruntled men before we were able to slay the traitors. In another version of events, Quintillus feared me so much that he opened his own veins, causing his men to fall on their swords in shame and dishonour.

To my ears the tales seemed hard to believe, but in their inebriated state, the men of the legions devoured it as the truth.

While the legionaries were deep into their cups, all of us congregated inside the pavilion vacated by Quintillus. It was a chilly spring evening and we huddled around glowing braziers while drinking heated wine.

"How did you know that Montanus and Florianus were commanding the legions?" I asked Hostilius.

"When I went to sacrifice at the bridge, I spoke with the peddler", Hostilius said. "He told me that the head centurions of the legions that had passed through, sacrificed at the altar. Both commissioned a stone and, as a sales ploy, he showed me the carvings."

"Where do we go from here, Lord Emperor?" Hostilius asked.

Although Quintillus was the one who murdered Marcus, I realised that he was but a tool in the hands of the Harbinger - the secret faction in the senate that wished to dominate and rule all.

I offered him a scowl. "We go to Rome, of course", I said. "And to make sure that the conscript fathers are well and truly committed to my rule, we take the two legions with us."

The Primus Pilus raised his cup in a gesture of support.

"Remember, Lucius of Da Qin, revenge not fix broken Empire", Cai cautioned.

Later, once all my friends had gone to their furs, I sat alone in the emperor's pavilion. Over the course of the evening the purple cloak had become increasingly heavy, until it felt as if it were woven of pure lead. I unclasped the fine garment and laid it over the back of a gold-embroidered couch. To my dismay, I found that the pressing weight of ultimate command remained.

Cai was right in his assertion that revenge would not mend the empire, but I chose not to heed his warning and decided to march on Rome. It might have been due to the fact that I believed that Marcus's death had not yet been fully avenged, or mayhap it was my hubris that sprouted from the fictitious sensation of unrestricted power.

In any event, it mattered not because the gods, who always wield the ultimate power, already had other plans.

* * *

The following morning, Diocles entered the pavilion before daybreak.

"Are you that eager to march on Rome?" I jested, but my aide's expression remained grim, indicating that something was amiss.

"A messenger arrived from Naissus", Diocles said. Moments later, he ushered an officer into the tent. The man appeared exhausted, was covered in dust and grime, and smelled of horse - there was no doubt in my mind that he had spent days in the saddle.

"Lord Emperor", the Illyrian decurion said, and bowed low.

I poured him a cup of watered wine with my own hand and waved him to his feet.

He accepted the proffered cup, nodded his appreciation, and thirstily gulped down the contents.

"Speak", I commanded.

"The Goths fell upon the Illyrian camp in Naissus, lord", he said. "We managed to repel the attack with few casualties, but the horde is swarming all over the countryside."

"And the Carpiani?" I asked.

"I am not sure on whose side the horse barbarians are, lord", he replied.

"Were you able to lay your hands on a prisoner?" I asked.

"One who spoke freely under torture", the decurion confirmed with a nod. "The Goth war chiefs have learned of the death of Emperor Claudius Gothicus. Once they heard that a senator, not a warrior, had claimed the purple, they were emboldened to go over onto the offensive." A slight smile played around the corners of the officer's lips as he finished his report.

"Do you find that amusing?" I asked.

His smile vanished. "No, Lord Emperor", he said. "It is just that… that if the barbarians knew who wears the purple, they would have stayed in the Haemus Mountains, even if it meant that they would starve."

* * *

I gestured for Diocles to remain while a praetorian escorted the decurion to his quarters for the evening. "Send him back the day after tomorrow with an escort of ten Illyrians", I said. "Draft orders that our scouts are to find the camp of the Goths. By the time we arrive at Naissus, I wish to know where the enemy is and how many warriors we will be facing."

"And", I added, "I wish to know the location of the Carpiani camp."

Diocles issued a curt nod and left the tent.

* * *

"We are leaving the borders of Raetia and Noricum open to invasion", Vibius said while glancing over his shoulder at the standard bearer who proudly held aloft his legion's gold eagle. The gilded oak staff was decorated with numerous *phalerae* as a reminder of their loyalty to the emperor. Behind him followed rank upon rank of legionaries marching in perfect step, their red shields bearing the famed white stork of the *Legio III Italica*.

"We need to put the Goths down once and for all", I said. "Besides, I doubt whether the Alemanni will be able to muster enough warriors to brush aside the auxiliary regiments that garrison the *limes*."

"You know how those savages are", Hostilius said. "By the time that their festering wounds are healed, they've drunk so much ale that their minds are addled good and proper. Then they imbibe some more and work up their courage to convince themselves that they have our measure. Before you know it, Braduhenna will have an army again."

"I have walked amongst the dead after the battle with the Germani", Gordas said. "We have decimated their clans. The few who have escaped will tell tales of carnage that will strike fear into the hearts of their warriors."

"I have received confirmation that the three legions that had spent the winter billeted at the forts of the Danube have arrived at Viminacium", Diocles confirmed. "They managed to bring their numbers up to full strength. Thanks to the spoils that we had taken last year at Naissus, they are well equipped and provisioned."

"Do you have a plan?" Hostilius asked.

The truth was that the Goth menace had to be dealt with decisively. If I allowed the barbarians to roam the hills of Thracia and Macedonia for another season or two, the legions would remain bogged down at Naissus. I was yet to decide on a strategy, but I knew that it would not do to appear indecisive.

"While our legions have recovered their strength, the Goths have been weakened by the winter spent in the Haemus Mountains", I said. "We will find their lair and fight them in the old way - by grinding them down with the might of our heavy infantry."

A smirk of satisfaction settled on Hostilius's face. "It's nothing fancy, but I like it", the Primus Pilus grunted. "I like it a lot."

Late afternoon we arrived in Sirmium. While the legions set up their camp beside the river, outside the walls, we rode on, having earlier decided to spend the evening at home.

Segelinde walked from the foyer of the villa just as I handed Kasirga's reins to a stable hand.

It was clear that the news of my ascension had reached her ears. "Lord Emperor", she said dutifully and made a curtsy.

"Lady Empress", I replied, and bowed low.

Although she issued a slight scowl, she came to me, wrapped her arms around my neck, and whispered into my ear. "Finally, you have embraced your destiny." She paused for a moment. "Did you kill Quintillus?" she asked.

I nodded.

"Good", the replied, and smiled sweetly.

We spent the evening around the dinner table, enjoying a simple meal of grilled fowl, freshly baked bread, soft cheese and sweet white wine. The food was good and the company even more so.

As the evening continued, I picked up on an uneasiness in Felix's manner. More than once I noticed him stroke the worn oak table with a calloused palm while gazing into the hearth fire. I would have dismissed it as melancholy that comes with old age if it were not for Adelgunde's unusual reservedness. I suspected that something was amiss.

The absence of Maximian and Nidada was not at all unusual as they spent most of their time with Pezhman who lived in a cabin in the hills to the north. Pezhman used to be a Sasanian slave, but now tended to the horse herds with the help of Hostilius's son and his adopted sibling.

"How are the boys doing?" Hostilius asked out of the blue - a not unusual question.

Adelgunde buried her head in her palms, issued a small shriek, and stormed off down the hallway. Felix averted his eyes, preferring to stare at the empty plate in front of him.

A deep frown settled on Hostilius's brow. He must also have noticed Felix's demeanour because he asked, "What aren't you telling me?"

"The boys are gone, centurion", Felix said.

"Gone?" Hostilius replied as he came to his feet. "What do you mean, 'gone'?"

It was Segelinde who came to Felix's rescue. "Sit down, centurion", she said. I recognised the tone - it was sufficient to cower the emperor of Rome, never mind Hostilius, who immediately retook his seat.

"Get the letter", she snapped at Felix. The oldster scampered from the room with an agility that belied his age, relieved to have been afforded the opportunity to escape Hostilius's ire.

Segelinde issued a sigh. "The boys have gone to join the legions", she said.

I noticed Hostilius's jaw drop.

Segelinde elbowed me in the ribs. "Close your mouth, you're gawking."

I did as I was told.

"It happened early in the new year", Segelinde continued. "Adelgunde blames Felix for putting the idea into their heads because he was the one who first helped them with their sword work and told them stories of life in the legions."

"What stories?" Hostilius asked, suddenly on his guard.

Her gaze alternated between us. "Stories about your adventures and exploits", she said, and I imagined that her voice carried an accusatory edge.

Just then Felix hobbled back into the room, a folded parchment in his hand.

Diocles accepted the letter with a nod.

Maximian to his father - many good wishes.

Nidada and I heard from our friends in the city that the Roman army is recruiting. Since I am eligible by birth and Nidada by adoption, we have decided to join the legions to defend the Empire against its enemies.

We do not wish to receive favour because of your or Uncle Lucius's standing in the legions, but want to prove ourselves by fighting in the ranks. We are travelling west, to Castra Regina, so that Nidada do not have to fight the warriors who were once his kinsmen.

If the gods will it, we will be promoted because you have brought us up well.

May Mars bless you.

Chapter 30 – Friend

"I will never understand women", Hostilius said, shaking his head. "All of us earn our living by defending the Empire with a sword in the hand. What in hades is wrong with that?"

"Women convince themselves that one can escape fate", Gordas growled. "They forget that death will find you even if you spend your whole life hiding in a marmot hole."

"Do you want me to write a letter of commendation for your sons, tribune?" Diocles asked Hostilius. "Mayhap we can ask the emperor to add his seal to it."

"There's an old saying in the legions", Hostilius said. "*If you want to live long enough to see retirement, keep your sword outside the scabbard and your tongue inside your mouth.*"

"Unlike sword, tongue of woman never rust", Cai remarked casually.

The Primus Pilus remained silent for a span of heartbeats, thinking on the Easterner's wisdom. Eventually he issued a sigh of defeat. "The problem is that once we're done with the Goths I will have to go home and face Adelgunde." He shrugged noncommittally and twisted to face Diocles. "Seeing that you want to help the boys, perhaps you can write to the commander of Castra Regina. Tell him that the emperor wants a list of all their new recruits and where they are doing duty. In that way I can put my wife's mind at ease without making a fuss."

"I will draft the missive this evening, as soon as we arrive at the fort at Viminacium", Diocles said. "And I will make sure it is dispatched at sunrise."

* * *

Early the following morning we departed from Viminacium, leading five legions south along the broad Via Militaris. I imagined that the giant oaks and beeches that flourished in the fertile soil on either side of the cobbles must already have been hundreds of years old when Emperor Traianus's legions toiled to turn a muddy barbarian track into a broad stone road. Gradually the road rose from the shadowy forest floor and ascended into the high country to bypass the worst of the swamps. From the path cut into the hillside we could see for miles.

Diocles allowed his eyes to wash over the seemingly endless sea of trees stretching in every direction. "They say that Rome has conquered these lands", he mused. "But I am sure that in this endless forest there are still wild men who have not even laid eyes upon a Roman."

Hostilius dismissed my aide's words with a flick of a hand. "Not true", he said, and took an *aureus* from his purse. "You see this. It lures savages like rotting meat attracts flies."

He had hardly spoken the words when there was a rustle in the undergrowth at the side of the road. Because of the Primus Pilus's assertion, I expected a tribesman to jump from the shrubs, but thankfully it was just a stag that darted across our path.

"I'll bet my last *sesterces* that the clans that hunt these forests sell furs at the markets in Viminacium or Naissus so they can lay their hands on Roman gold. And just like that", he added and snapped his fingers, "they have a new master."

"Let me ask you another thing", Hostilius said, getting into his stride. "Whose face is on this coin?"

"The Roman emperor's, of course", Diocles replied reservedly, suspecting a trap.

"Exactly!" the Primus Pilus exclaimed. "You see, once the tribes have fallen for the glitter of our coin they are already slaves of the Empire, they just don't realise it."

Hostilius was right, of course. Many men north and south of the Danube had unknowingly been enslaved by the allure of coin.

* * *

Early afternoon five days later, we left the murky gloom of the forest behind, crossed the Roman bridge, and marched the legions onto the plain where we had destroyed the great army of the Goths.

I felt a pang of sadness when I realised that Marcus had still been with us when we had last been to Naissus but a handful of months before. I suspected that my friends were also reliving the battle in their minds, so it came as no surprise when the conversation died down as we trotted across the green pastureland that had not long before been saturated with blood.

Approaching the small bridge that led to the fort, Hostilius turned his face away from me. "Marcus was a good friend. I miss him", he whispered, his voice hoarse with emotion.

"I do too", I replied, and drew a deep breath to regain my composure before the massive gates creaked open.

* * *

The following morning, while it was still dark, Hostilius and three scouts followed me through a sally gate in the wall. Twenty paces away, Gordas, who had spent the night in the Illyrian camp, was waiting with our horses.

The Hun issued an offhanded grunt, handed out the reins, and gained the saddle with an agility usually reserved for the young.

"Where is Vibius?" Hostilius asked as he passed me a chunk of dried beef.

"Vibius is inspecting the legionary camps", I said, and tore at the meat with my teeth.

"And the Greek?" he asked.

"He is dispatching correspondence all across the Empire", I said.

"Your orders?" the Primus Pilus asked.

"Mostly his", I replied. "He knows the workings of the state inside and out. I fear that I am the Emperor in all but name.

Diocles and his team of scribes and army of functionaries run the Empire."

"That boy's got a good head on his shoulders", Hostilius said. "We have a lot on our plates as it is, fighting the enemies of Rome and all. I agree - leave the paperwork to the Greek. If anybody can fix half a century of mismanagement, its him."

* * *

The sun had already emerged above the peaks when we approached a rocky hilltop. We dismounted and the scout gestured to a crooked black alder that straddled the crest. "There is cover over there, lord", he said.

Through the curtain of branches we saw the sprawling Goth camp far below in the broad valley of the Nisava River. "How many?" I asked.

"We cannot be sure, lord emperor", he replied, rubbing his stubbled chin. "But we estimate ninety thousand warriors."

I noticed a band of horsemen, mayhap five hundred, approach from the east along the valley floor. "More of them arrive every day, lord", the scout said. "I think the new war chief has united the wayward clans."

"We managed to destroy an army of two hundred thousand savages", Hostilius said. "We can sure as hades defeat an army of a hundred thousand."

"Last time we had help", I said. "May I remind you that it was the arrow storm of the Scythians that kept the enemy at bay. The final charge of their heavy cavalry was the straw that broke the Goths' back."

"Maybe", the Primus Pilus admitted grudgingly.

"And this time there will be no help from Octar or the easterners who wield the tiger bow", Gordas said, adding weight to my argument.

"Even though they will be outnumbered two to one, the legions and the Illyrians might win the day", I admitted. "But if we lose half our army in the battle we will be overrun by the next enemy waiting in line. We need mounted archers."

"The Roxolani?" Hostilius asked.

"Aritê and the wolf warriors of Naulobates are engaged in the far north of her realm", I said. "Burdukhan said that she is visiting her wrath upon the hillmen. Knowing my daughter, I am sure it will be a long and bloody campaign."

* * *

The following morning, the sun was only a double handspan above the eastern horizon when I ducked into the tent of Thiaper, the king of the Carpiani.

"You come to the tent of a horse barbarian even though you are the king of the Romans?" he asked.

"Do I look like the Roman emperor?" I said.

Earlier that morning I had donned the horse-hoof scale armour that Bradakos had gifted me all those years before. A fine-woven wool cloak was draped over my shoulders. The crimson material was embroidered with intricate gold stitching, depicting a royal hunt. My undyed leather *braccae* were workmanlike, but my soft deerskin riding boots and matching leather belt adorned with gold plaques showed that I was a Scythian noble of the highest order.

Thiaper shook his head in answer, a slight smile playing around the corners of his mouth.

"Can Eochar of the Roxolani not visit and old friend?" I asked.

"You are welcome at my hearth, Prince Eochar", he replied, and waved the two burly guards from our presence.

I sat down cross-legged on the furs beside the hearth and watched as the king decanted fresh mare's milk into a small copper pot which he placed onto the glowing embers. While the milk warmed, he took a leather satchel from his belt and added coarse salt to the brew, then a dollop of fresh butter.

I took a sip of the scalding liquid, rich and salty, and closed my eyes to savour the taste. "I feel like a boy receiving salted milk from the hand of his father", I said.

"You are truly a man of the Sea of Grass", the king said, and chuckled. "Who would have thought that a Scythian would sit on the Roman throne."

"We all bend to the will of Arash, do we not?" I replied.

"Speaking of the god", he said, and gestured to my red cloak. "I see that you wear the colour of war."

"War is upon us", I replied, and took another sip.

"Three days ago, I was visited by the war chief of the Goths", Thiaper said, and refilled my cup. "The one they call Little Wolf. He claims that you murdered his father."

"What do you think?" I asked.

"I care not for the fate of Tharuarus", Thiaper replied. "Ulfilas wants an alliance against Rome. He told me that the man who wears the purple is no warrior, a weakling who can hardly wield a blade."

I took another sip of milk.

"He offered to divide these lands amongst the Goths and Carpiani", Thiaper said. "It is a tempting offer for one who has no lands. An offer that warrants serious consideration."

I grunted my agreement.

Thiaper's lips curled up in a savage leer. "But then I heard that the weakling Emperor had been vanquished and that Eochar the Merciless, the warrior who walks in the shadow of the lord of blood, has claimed the Roman throne."

He sipped from his own cup.

"Even if you were not my friend, I would not be fool enough to join a doomed cause", he said.

"Seeing that you have rejected the offer of the Goths, are you willing to fight at my side instead?" I asked.

"The Carpiani is a tribe without a home", he said, staring into the fire. "Soon, we will journey through the mountains to take our flocks across the Mother River. We have decided to go far to the north, beyond the reach of the Crow, and with our sword arms and our bows we will carve out a new homeland. I cannot waste the lives of my men."

I made to offer a counter argument, but Thiaper raised an open palm. "Do not offer to pay us more gold", he said. "We have enough. Unlike the Goths, we did not have to hide in the mountains during the winter to escape the wrath of Rome. My warriors hunted the forests and our wagons are filled with joints of smoked venison and salted boar. Our flocks of sheep and herds of cattle and horses have grown fat grazing the sweet grass of these fertile lands. We are preparing to go north and want no more part in the battles of Rome. You are wasting your time, Eochar. You will always be a friend, but there is nothing that you can say or do that will change my mind."

Then the god whispered into my ear.

The emperor of Rome said his piece and gained nearly six thousand horse archers for the inevitable battle against the Goths.

Chapter 31 – Dice (May 270 AD)

Vibius and Diocles stared at me in a way that suggested that I had lost my mind.

I was almost certain that Cai was suppressing a slight smile, but one never knew for sure with the Easterner.

Gordas paid me no heed and continued to clean his nails with the tip of his dagger. His reaction came as no surprise as the Huns placed little value in borders. His kind freely roamed the steppes in search of pasture for their herds, often forcing weaker or less warlike tribes to abandon their ancestral land and run for the hills.

"You did what?" Hostilius said once he had managed to close his mouth.

"I have secured the services of the Carpiani for a year", I replied, and took another swig of wine.

"It is wise", Gordas said, satisfied that my decision was strategically sound.

Hostilius chugged the contents of his cup. "I was talking about the first part of the sentence, Domitius", Hostilius remarked.

"That part where I promised the Roman province of Dacia to the Carpiani in exchange for them fighting at our side?" I asked innocently.

"I thought that we are trying to restore the Empire to its former glory", he said, scowling. "Now you hand out what little land we have left to the savages."

"If we fail to destroy the Goths, the Empire is no more", I replied. "And if we lose too many men, we will struggle to rebuild the decimated legions. Besides, Gallienus has already stripped Dacia of its defences, and barbarian clans continually raid the frontier lands. At least with new masters, the Romans who choose to remain there will be protected. The ones who do not will be granted lands in the provinces decimated by years of war."

I looked Hostilius straight in the eye. "Would you send the Carpiani home if it were your decision? Could you defend Dacia against the hordes of the Crow with the remnants of the border garrisons?"

The Primus Pilus took thirty heartbeats to digest my words.

"Probably not", he said, his scowl deepening. "But that doesn't make it any more palatable to know that you're giving away hard-won land."

"Sometimes the gods demand a sacrifice of something dear before they bestow their favour", I said. "Dacia was the sacrifice that they wished for."

My friends were aware of the fact that the god of war and fire spoke to me on occasion. Although I did not reveal it, they accepted my words with nods all around.

"It matters not, the die is cast", I said. "I have given my word to Thiaper. Let us not waste our breath on arguing the merits of my decision, but rather use the time at our disposal to prepare for war."

* * *

Three weeks later, on the eve of the start of the campaign, Hostilius strolled into my quarters while Diocles and I were corresponding with the provinces. I noticed that the Primus Pilus had two *sagums* draped over a thick forearm, one of which he presented to me.

"Come, Domitius", he said, and gestured to the oiled cloaks. "It's drizzling outside, so no one will give us a second glance if we wander about the camp."

"I am dictating a letter to the governor of Hispania", I said.

Hostilius dismissed my words with a flick of a hand. "I'm sure the Greek's better at it than you are", he replied. "Leave him to do it himself."

I noticed a look pass between my two friends, causing me to suspect that they had connived behind my back.

"I know what needs to be done, Lord Emperor", Diocles volunteered drily, confirming my suspicion that I was more of a distraction than a help when it came to matters of politics.

I donned the hooded garment, waved away the protests of the praetorians, and followed Hostilius into the night.

The guards at the gate fell over their feet to open the door as soon as the Primus Pilus flicked back the hood of his *sagum*. They knew better than to ask a senior tribune, who also happened to be a confidant of the emperor, to identify his companion.

"Let's start with the *Legio II Italica*", Hostilius said, and strolled to where a large, torch-lit banner depicted the famed she-wolf suckling the twins Romulus and Remus.

Since the times of the great Manius Dentatus, every Roman legionary camp had been set out in the same way. Hostilius and I had spent half our lives with the legions and we had no trouble locating the rows of tents housing the soldiers. Outside the goatskin shelters, the men of the *contubernia* huddled around small wood fires, cooking their evening meals. The icy drizzle continued unabated and all wore their hooded cloaks.

Hostilius strolled closer to a tent group and produced a dice box from underneath his *sagum*. "Would you be interested in a game of dice, friends?" he asked.

At first we received no reply, the men eyeing us with a healthy dose of suspicion bordering on hostility. Eventually a scarred veteran, most probably the *decanus*, spoke up. "I don't know you, strangers", he said. "Get you gone."

But the Primus Pilus knew soldiers better that he knew himself. He produced an amphora from behind his back, one that I immediately recognised as originating from the imperial cellar. Hostilius used the amphora to gesture in my direction. "I guess that the second of the third will be more interested in tasting the falernian that Lucius here happened to get his hands on", he said, and made to turn to a nearby tent. Looking over his shoulder, he added, "We can't share it with our comrades in the *VII Claudia* 'cause they know our faces, and this amphora is stamped with the imperial seal. We can't have it all cause tomorrow we're going into battle and we need our wits about us."

Even I knew that wine of the quality that Hostilius carried would probably set a legionary back a full year's pay.

"Maybe we've judged you too harshly, friends", the *decanus* called out, raising a palm in a placating gesture. "Truth is, we've had men here before selling falernian. It turned out that they swapped it with soured wine - the kind that I won't even dish out to our section slaves. Now, you don't happen to be like those men, eh?"

Hostilius handed the sealed amphora to the junior officer who reverently accepted it, handling it as a mother would her babe. "Why don't you pour yourself a cup and taste it."

Barely able to contain his excitement, the *decanus* pried open the waxed stopper, poured himself a brimming cup and took a deep swallow. He gave Hostilius an incredulous look, passed the cup to one of his men, and gestured for his friends to make room for us beside the cooking fire.

"What should we play for?" one of the soldiers asked while he poured thin, sloppy dough into an oiled skillet.

"By the end of the week we might all be in Elysium. I say we keep our coin in our purses for the funeral fund", Hostilius said. "Why don't we rather take turns to gamble for a sip of falernian. The man who comes up Venus can have two swallows but if you throw dogs, you pass."

Hostilius's suggestion was met by grunts of approval.

"You boys worried about tomorrow?" Hostilius asked after coming up dogs for the second time in three turns.

"Where in hades have you two been the past three years?" the officer chuckled.

"The last time me and Lucius here stood in the ranks, it was for Gallienus", Hostilius said. "Since then, we've been garrisoning a fort in the middle of the bloody Danube. We've only been recalled recently."

The *decanus*, who was called Attius, shook his head in a gesture of sympathy. "We've fought for Emperor Claudius Gothicus. He was a good soldier and it's a right shame that he's gone. But by the gods, the new emperor is a proper warrior. I spoke to a man who used to serve with him when he was in the ranks. Lucius Domitius is a killer, and what is more, the gods love him. There ain't a man in the legions who thinks otherwise."

He paused, squinting in the low light to see how the dice had fallen. In delight Attius slapped his knee with an open palm as all four of the little cubes landed on a different number, eliciting moans from all around the fire. I poured two swallows and passed him the cup.

"Do you think we'll get to kick the Goths' arses?" Hostilius asked, and nodded his thanks as a legionary handed him a folded chickpea pancake.

"We'll kick their arses good and proper, don't you worry", Attius said. "Only problem is that some of the men are worried that the savages will turn and make a run for it when they see Lucius Domitius at the head of the legions."

"Is that so bad?" Hostilius asked.

"If there's no battle, there's no loot", the *decanus* replied. Then he gestured to me. "Your friend doesn't talk much, eh?"

"He prefers to use his blade instead of his tongue", Hostilius said, and issued a chuckle as he came up dogs again.

Chapter 32 – Haemus Mountains

Early on the morrow, I led the army east. We followed the course of the Nisava into the mountains of Thracia, marching along the northern bank.

Hostilius glanced at the never-ending column of legionaries trailing us. "It'll go well - the boys are behind you all the way, Domitius", he said.

"How did you manage to throw so many dogs?" I asked, referring to the Primus Pilus's uncanny bad fortune during the previous evening's game with Attius's *contubernium*.

"The dice are loaded, of course", Hostilius said as if it were the most natural thing in the world. "I took it off a legionary years ago when we served in Germania."

"Why would one wish to load dice so that it comes up dogs?" Vibius asked, referring to the unfortunate instance when all four dice landed on the number one.

"The bastard fleeced a lot of my men", he said. "Until I realised that he used two sets of loaded dice. One when he wanted to lose and another when he wanted to win."

"You see", Hostilius mused. "When playing dice, it's no good winning all the time. If you lose, or fake losing, it puts the others at ease and before they know it, you've emptied their purses."

"Or that's what I've been told", he added as an afterthought before Diocles or Vibius could comment on his in-depth knowledge of a frowned-upon pastime.

"Where is the set of winning dice?" Diocles asked.

"Where do you think?" Hostilius replied with a mischievous grin.

Hostilius's words milled around inside my head. I believe to this day that it was a message sent by Arash.

Cai, who accompanied us to help tend to the wounded, must have noticed my sudden silence. "Dice much like war", he said. "When strong, best appear weak."

Cai was right, of course. But his wisdom was not so easy to translate into actions. "The Goths may outnumber us", I said, "but they know that five legions are a formidable force. They are aware of our numbers. It is impossible to hide the legions from their scouts who are surely crawling all over these hills."

"I not emperor", Cai said. "I find way to heal wounded. You find way to look weak, Lucius of Da Qin."

I believe I must have scowled.

* * *

"Lord Emperor", the outrider said, and inclined his head.

I indicated for the decurion to report.

"The camp of the Goths lies ten miles east, on this side of the river", he said. "Their camp is a hive of activity."

"Are they vulnerable to a cavalry attack?" I asked.

The decurion shook his head. "No, lord, the front of their camp is fortified by a ring of ox wagons. Every wagon bristles with spears - some are fitted with whetted iron, while most are sharpened stakes hardened by fire. The rear of their camp is protected by the Nisava which is sixty paces wide, deep and in full flow."

"Where is the closest ford?" I asked.

"Seven miles to the east there is a narrow shelf of rock that lies just beneath the surface", he said, indicating the river. "On the other side of the crossing is a forested path that leads back to Naissus. A few hundred men can cross with ease, lord, but… but it will take time for a legion to get to the other side."

"Report to the engineering corps and lead them to the ford", I said. "I will join you soon."

"I understand and I will obey, Lord Emperor", he said, saluted in the way of the legions, and turned his mount around to do my bidding.

* * *

The grizzled head of the engineering corps ran his fingers through his short-cropped hair and shared a look with another grey-haired veteran. "Lord", he said, in an effort to be as diplomatic as possible, "your required specifications are highly irregular."

"Yes", I sighed, as I had expected his reaction.

"If it is too much of an ask, I will get the head centurions of the legions to order their men to slap together something workable", Hostilius suggested.

A frown of concern furrowed the engineer's brow, undoubtedly fearing being shown up by uneducated men. "Of course we can build it", he said. "It is just that…"

I held up an open palm. "Good", I said. "I will inspect the completed works before sunset."

"It will be done, lord", the man said, and bowed as I swung onto Kasirga's back.

* * *

Later that evening, once I was satisfied that my instructions were adhered to, I retired to my pavilion. The perimeter walls of the camp had been laid out in the shape of a U, with the open side abutting the northern bank of the river. Contrary to regulations there was no earthen rampart facing the ford in the Nisava. To ensure that we would not be overrun from the unfortified side, Diocles arranged for a full cohort to guard the crossing at all times.

In addition, I had ordered the engineers to break through the bank of the river so that the water flooded the deep ditch and surrounded the camp on three sides, apart from the gates in the northern wall, of course.

"I've been marching under the eagle since I was sixteen", Hostilius said that evening, a cup of wine in his hand. "But I've never heard of a ditch on the inside of the walls of a legionary camp. If it were anyone else…", he added with a shake of his head, "but I know Mars speaks to you, Domitius."

"We will find out soon", I said, emptied my cup, and stood to retire to my furs.

While I drifted off to sleep, I could still hear the hammer blows of the army of workmen toiling into the night. They were building the wooden bridges that would allow the men to cross the V-shaped ditch and man the ramparts in case the Goths attacked. I wondered whether I had misinterpreted the signs of the gods and whether I would leave the valley of the Nisava a hero or a corpse.

* * *

As soon as it was light enough to march, I led the army east. Unlike a normal Roman camp, all four gates were situated close together in the northern wall that faced away from the river.

Two-thirds of a watch later, we deployed the legions in battle formation, three hundred paces from where the Goth horde was assembling.

"Where is the Hun?" Hostilius asked.

"He is with Thiaper of the Carpiani", I replied.

"And Vibius and the Greek?" he asked.

"Vibius is in the camp to make sure that the *immunes* do what they are supposed to do, and Diocles is leading the Illyrians", I replied.

"Do the legions know exactly what is expected of them?" I asked Hostilius.

"That must be the tenth time you've asked me", the Primus Pilus replied.

"Humour your emperor", I said.

"They all know what to do", he said. "I have spoken with all the head centurions several times. I can't say they're elated, but they'll follow you all the way through the black gates of Hades, even if you happen to cheat your way past Cerberus."

"Good", I replied. "Because that's what we are about to do."

* * *

The standard bearer raised the golden image of the emperor. A heartbeat later, the shrill notes of a *buccina* echoed from the hills and rolled down the valley.

Three hundred banners, one for each century in the army, were lifted high. Some of the hafts of the standards were topped with leaf-shaped blades while others carried the sculpted image of the open hand which showed the soldiers' loyalty to their emperor. Thirty thousand legionaries clad in chain and scale hefted their *scuta* and took the first steps towards the spear-bristling ranks of chanting barbarians.

Ten thousand Illyrians were drawn up behind the legions, ready to repel an attack from the Goth medium cavalry who were milling about at the rear of the barbarian ranks. The enemy, I hoped, did not know that Thiaper had chosen to throw in his fate with Rome. For that reason I had ensured that the Carpiani remained out of sight.

When forty paces separated the armies, thousands of projectiles were hurled into the air. Spears rained down on the ranks of Romans and Goths alike, but because of their superior armour and training, fewer legionaries succumbed in the onslaught.

From fifty paces behind our front rank, I watched as the two armies collided. The Goths, on average, were large men, tall and heavily muscled. But what the Romans lacked in sheer bulk, they made up for in training. Since the start of Marcus's reign, when he had given me control of the armies of Rome, I had ensured that the legionaries honed their skills through mock battles where centuries, and even cohorts, regularly faced one another shield to shield.

I heard the familiar sound as the Roman *scuta* creaked under the strain of a hundred thousand Goth warriors. Lodging their round shields against ours, they pushed and heaved with all their might, but the legions stood their ground.

Slowly but inexorably the Roman line started to bend under the enormous pressure. The shouts of optios and centurions rallying their centuries competed with the screams of barbarian champions defying the might of Rome.

Hostilius watched the battle unfold with the eye of an expert. "Another fifty heartbeats and the line will break", he said. "If they pour into our ranks, we're done for."

"Do it", I said.

The *buccina* relayed my orders to the legions. As one, the Roman ranks shuffled backwards, dressing the line in the process.

A roar of triumph rose from the horde. Invigorated by their success, the men of the tribes surged forward to vanquish a foe that none could overcome in a thousand years.

Again, the Roman line bent under the barbarian onslaught.

I looked to Hostilius for guidance. He issued a grim nod. "It is time", he said.

"Signal the orderly retreat", I commanded. "The legions are to fall back to the marching camp."

In response to my words, a sorrowful wail echoed down the valley.

Chapter 33 – Hannibal

Sensing victory in the Roman retreat, the chieftains roused their men into a crazed frenzy of attack. But the soldiers in the front ranks of the legions were the victors of the Battle of Naissus - the rock-hard warriors of the frontline cohorts who had faced worse odds, and lived to tell the tale. With shields drawn tight against their shoulders they shuffled backwards, fending off the onslaught like cliffs that stand proud against the might of thundering waves.

Overeager to vanquish the enemy, the tribesmen were the ones who suffered most. Baying for Roman blood, Goth warriors trampled their wounded brethren who had succumbed to the biting blades of *gladii*. As the horde advanced, they left behind a grim carpet of dead and dying.

Above the barbarian chants and screams that threatened to overpower my very thoughts, rose the booming voices of centurions, who by the sheer power of their will, kept their men from turning their backs to the foe. The standard bearers held the Roman banners high - a sign that the legions were far from being defeated.

"By the gods, there are many of them", Hostilius said when the battle had raged for nearly a watch. "I just hope we make it back to the ramparts before the boys are too tired to lift their blades."

And then we sighted the wooden towers on the walls of the marching camp. To facilitate a retreat through the gates, I signalled for the two legions farthest from the centre to close their ranks and narrow their frontage.

Unavoidably, the manoeuvre opened gaps on both flanks. The Goth horsemen immediately jumped at the opportunity. Twenty thousand mounted spearmen split into equal groups and thundered towards the gaps, eager to fall on the flanks of the legions.

But Diocles's Illyrians were moving even before the legions had executed my orders. As the gaps appeared, the Roman horsemen spurred their mounts from a trot to a canter. When the mob of Goth cavalry first laid eyes on the Illyrians, their fate was sealed. The heavily armoured black riders thundered down on them in perfectly dressed ranks, their long lances held horizontal.

The enemy riders hesitated, allowing the Illyrians to slam into an almost stationary foe, spilling over them like a dark tide. The black-clad riders did not rein in, but charged into the flanks of the horde, their spears reaping tribesmen by the hundreds.

Barbarian war horns blared, and in response the Goth infantry disengaged to regroup, allowing the exhausted legions to continue their retreat unmolested.

Rather than pushing their advantage, the Illyrians withdrew from the battlefield.

* * *

Much later, Hostilius, Vibius and I stood in one of the defensive towers lining the northern wall of the marching camp. Five hundred paces distant, the Goth horde was milling about.

Hostilius leaned forward, his calloused palms pressing against the rough-hewn oak railing. "It doesn't seem like there are fewer of them than this morning", he said as he squinted at the host surrounding the camp.

Just then Diocles arrived. He walked across the makeshift bridge, scampered up the ladder to gain the top of the rampart, and then up another set of rungs to join us in the tower.

"Report, tribune", I said, acknowledging him with a nod.

"The legions suffered two hundred and thirty-four casualties, while six hundred and five of our men are wounded and unfit for duty", Diocles said. "Sixty-two Illyrians were wounded but none lost their lives."

He paused to accept a wax tablet from a junior tribune.

"If I collate the numbers, the Goths lost nearly four thousand five hundred men", he said. "It is significant."

"Still doesn't look like it", Hostilius said, his eyes fixed on the regrouping horde.

"Do you think they will attack?" my aide asked.

"They believe that they have hurt us", Hostilius said. "They are like wolves who have tasted blood. Oh yes, they will try one more time before sunset."

"We have assembled a *carroballista* in every one of the forty towers", Vibius said, and ran his fingers through his hair in an attempt rid himself of more saw dust. "Dealing with the engineers was as tough as fighting barbarians, but eventually we made all the modifications you asked for."

I nodded my appreciation of his efforts. "Have the ballistae been tested and ranged?" I asked.

"They have", Vibius confirmed, and accepted a cup from the hand of a servant. "Three of them draw their bolts a few feet to the right, but the crews will compensate."

"The Illyrians?" I asked Diocles.

"They have retreated seven miles up the valley and are concealed in the beech forest bordering the road", he said. "I have ordered that no fires be lit, and they will set a triple line of pickets around their camp just in case the Goths launch a surprise attack or try to scatter the horses. As far as the enemy is concerned, the Illyrians have fled the field and returned to the safety of their camp at Naissus."

"Here they come", Hostilius said, his eyes never having left the horde.

"Do the crews of the ballistae in the towers know that they must stay their hands?" I asked.

"They have their orders", Vibius confirmed, "and will not engage."

Never in a thousand years had a Roman marching camp been overrun by barbarians. I was not planning to go down in history as the first emperor to oversee such a catastrophe. But neither did I wish to destroy the Goths' belief that they could emerge victorious.

"I don't like it that you're only sending one of the five legions to defend the wall", Hostilius grumbled as hundreds of legionaries of the *Legio II Italica* scampered up the ladders that led to the rampart. "I know what you want to do, and why you are doing it, but you're playing with fire, Domitius."

"If we merely defeat the Goths like we did at Naissus, it will not be enough", I sighed. "While we hunt the thousands who escape our blades, what remains of the Empire will slowly wither away. Overmorrow, when the sun rises, I will either be strolling through the fields of Elysium, or the Goths will be tamed."

"Well, I guess Fortuna favours the brave", Hostilius relented with a shrug.

"Actually, Fortuna favours the virtuous", Diocles corrected the Primus Pilus.

"Same thing", Hostilius said, and raised his shield to deflect a spear that would have pinned me to the wood.

* * *

It was dusk when the barbarians finally broke off their attack. They had managed to breach our thin defences in a number of places to gain footholds on the rampart. The timeous and ferocious intervention of the frontline centuries of the other legions that were kept in reserve, soon reduced the cheering champions to corpses that littered the area in front of the wall.

After retreating to a safe distance, the Goths did not immediately skulk back to their camp. They jeered and taunted the legionaries who silently watched from the walls. The barbarians shouted insults, telling us that they would be back the following morning to finish what they had started. Their actions clearly showed that they were not disheartened, but rather hungry for victory.

When the darkness was thick around us, I went to find Hostilius, who was overseeing the evacuation of the camp. By the light of Mani, cohort after cohort, aligned in double column order, waded through the icy water along the narrow shelf that spanned the Nisava. The Primus Pilus had spun two ropes across the river to demarcate the position of the crossing. Ten paces from where we stood on the bank, a legionary stepped out of line. His left foot slipped off the edge of the shelf, and with a muffled cry he was taken by the dark water. A comrade thrust the haft of his pilum into the murky blackness and managed to fish the fortunate soldier from his doom.

"By the gods", Hostilius hissed. "Watch what you're doing. The next fool to step off the path will be on latrine duty for the remainder of his time under the standard. And for the sake of hades, get moving. You're strolling like a bunch of Vestal Virgins on their way to a festival."

Immediately the legionaries moved closer together and their pace picked up. Hostilius was not known for idle threats.

"How many have crossed?" I asked.

"This is the ninth cohort of the first legion to cross", Hostilius said. "There are still a lot who's got to get their feet wet."

"Will they get across before first light?" I asked.

"If they don't make it across the river before then, it's fine by me. I'll just let the ones who remain swim the current", he said loud enough for the men to hear.

Again, the pace picked up.

Chapter 34 – Camp

At the grey hour of the wolf, Hostilius slashed the ropes that demarcated the ford. Before relinquishing his post, the Primus Pilus turned around to make sure that he was the last man who remained in the marching camp. Satisfied, he swung up into the saddle and coaxed his mount into the river.

While we waited on the southern bank for Hostilius's horse to pick its way across the ford, I took in the sorry scene. It was evident that the legions had abandoned their camp in a hurry. Hundreds of wagons, some with missing wheels, others with broken axles, were scattered around the area. Most were still stacked with provisions that the legions needed on a daily basis - amphorae of wine and olive oil, bags of wheat flour and bundles of dry firewood. There were even a few goats and sheep roaming around untended. I could not help but smile as I noticed the odd cartload of *pilum* hafts and iron ingots that Vibius had haphazardly strewn about for good measure.

My friend issued a broad grin, as he was the one charged with creating the impression that the legions had run away during the hours of darkness. "Convincing, eh?" he said. "In fact, it is so believable, I have to continually remind myself that we are not really running away with our tail between our legs."

I twisted in the saddle to study the road that led south, back to Naissus. Half a mile down the track, Vibius had arranged a dozen wagons stacked with amphorae of wine. Just beyond the wagons, the tail end of the marching column was visible. "If the Goths are not baited by the stragglers of the *VII Claudia*, the wine will lure them", he stated with confidence.

At that moment, Hostilius joined us, his horse powering up the bank onto solid ground. "The wine will do the trick", he said, having picked up on the tail end of the conversation. "If there's one thing savages enjoy more than killing, it's drinking themselves into a stupor." The Primus Pilus gestured at the eastern horizon. "We'd better get under cover of the trees before they see us. They might be barbarians, but that doesn't mean they're stupid."

We entered the shadows on the left side of the dirt track and picked our way a few paces into the gloom. At first, all we could discern was a low murmur of voices and the odd flash as a blade was illuminated by a shivelight. As our eyes became accustomed to the darkness, we noticed two wolf-cloaked standard bearers holding aloft gold eagles. Behind them, the forest of beech and oak was teeming with men - twelve thousand soldiers of the second and third Italian legions arrayed in attack formation. On the opposite side of the road, another two full legions lurked amongst the trees, ready to fall upon the right flank of the men pursuing the *Legio VII Claudia*.

As the sun peeked out behind the mountains, I nudged Kasirga to the edge of the trees. Already, thousands of Goths were streaming through the open gates in the northern wall of the abandoned Roman camp. Like ants swarming a pot of honey, the barbarians clustered around the loot.

None seemed to notice the wide moat that lined the inside of the walls. So focused was the enemy on plunder that no one paused to study the stake-lined palisade where the sharpened lengths of timber curiously pointed inwards. They also did not find it strange that the heavy towers had no access ladders or that the thick beams of the gates were gleaming with oil.

Across the water I spied a chieftain on a large stallion, his back facing the ford. I was certain that it was Ulfilas, the war chief himself. "Leave the food for the women and children", he roared, his longsword pointing rearward at the ford in the river. "We will catch the Romani in the open and destroy them. Tonight, you will all have a set of good armour and an iron shortsword in your belt. Their lands will be at our mercy. We will plunder the Eternal City where the streets are paved with gold."

"Paved with gold, eh?" Hostilius said from beside me. "More like paved with s…" An almighty roar emanated from the host on the other side of the river, drowning out the conversation.

"Here they come", Vibius said.

The first few Goths to wade in were no fools, cautiously picking their way across until they had established the width of the ford. Then the floodgates opened and hundreds of barbarian warriors powered through the shallows to join their leader on the southern bank of the river. When the mob was twenty thousand strong, Ulfilas raised his sword and pointed the blade to where the stragglers of the *VII Claudia* were disappearing around a far bend in the track. "Kill the Romani and you will be rich beyond your dreams", he boomed.

Like hounds obeying their master, the mob lurched forward.

In the distance I heard the call of the *buccina*. In response, the marching legion halted and deployed across the hundred-pace-wide open ground to receive the attack of the Goths. There was a dull thud as the advance of the foe was checked by the plywood shields of the iron-clad men of the *VII Claudia*.

Still, tribesman continued to pour across the river while even greater numbers were entering through the northern gates, causing the Roman camp to fill up.

Suddenly there was a commotion at the far side of the Roman fortifications as thousands of the enemy rushed to get into the camp.

"I haven't seen so many men trying to get through a gate since the time you fought in the Flavian Amphitheatre during Rome's thousand-year celebrations", Vibius jested.

A great cloud of dust rose from beyond the wall and I knew that it was the handiwork of my aide. He was leading the Illyrians in an attack against the rearguard of the Goths, effectively herding them into the camp. When the stream petered out, bright orange flames engulfed the gates as Diocles's horsemen sealed the openings with bundles of burning brushwood. Within thirty heartbeats, the oil-soaked timber of the gates were aflame. The heavy oak beams would burn for at least a watch and the embers would remain for another, effectively barring the Goths inside the camp.

From beyond the walls we heard the thunder of hooves and screams of the dying as the Illyrians fell on the enemy warriors who had been too slow to reach safety.

To our left, the men of the *VII Claudia* were fighting for their lives. Inexorably, they were being pushed back by the sheer weight of the Goths, their numbers having swelled to close on thirty thousand. Barbarians were still crossing the river, although many were glancing over their shoulders at the burning gates and the thick black smoke billowing into the sky.

It was time.

The shrill note of the *buccina* was followed by a primal roar as twenty-four thousand legionaries stormed from the cover of the trees, casting their pila as they sprang the trap. Thousands of the enemy died without having laid eyes on their vanquishers. Five heartbeats later, the legions slammed into the decimated flanks of the Goths.

The tide turned almost immediately. Literally and figuratively.

The mob, realising that they had been tricked, turned tail and rushed back to the river crossing, desperately trying to escape their doom. But the ford could only accommodate so many at one time. Hundreds, if not thousands, were pushed over the edge and claimed by the raging waters, the weight of their arms and armour dragging them to a watery grave.

I saw a mounted Ulfilas powering through the shallows, his large stallion trampling the unfortunate men who happened to be in his path.

On the northern bank of the river the Goths licked their wounds while the legions lined up on the southern bank. Although at least ten thousand had perished in the ambush, there were still more than eighty thousand men milling about inside the Roman camp.

I walked my horse to the muddy bank. Across the river, fifty paces distant, Ulfilas sat on his stallion.

"You and your legions will die for this treachery", he fumed, his blade pointed at me. "You are too weak to face us in battle. But you made a mistake. We have claimed your camp and your supplies."

"May I?" Vibius said from beside me.

"Be my guest", I replied.

The *buccina's* thrill note travelled across the river to the far side of the earthen embankment. Moments later, thousands of warriors appeared on the ramparts. Some wielded horn bows and wore the garb of Scythians, while others were clad in burnished black armour and carried quivers of war darts. Gordas had brought the Carpiani to join the Illyrians on the wall.

"It is not a camp", I shouted to Ulfilas. "It is a cage."

The war chief shouted a command and thousands of his men charged the wall. But there were no wooden bridges across the moat. The Goths struggling through the mud were slain by arrows and war darts, and the handful who managed to clamber up the ramparts were impaled on Illyrian lances.

I raised my right arm.

In response, a three-foot-long iron-tipped haft slammed into the water, five paces in front of Ulfilas.

Little Wolf twisted in the saddle, his gaze drifting across the forty wooden towers from where the whetted heads of bolts were pointing menacingly at the horde.

"You are a coward, Roman", he screeched. "Just like you stabbed my father in the back, you will kill us from a distance with your machines of death."

"You are a liar and a murderer, Goth", I said. "I only wish for you to stop ravaging the lands of my people." I indicated the host. "Amongst your warriors there are many who fought in the armies of Kniva, a man whom I called friend."

A murmur of consent rose from the mob.

Hostilius must have divined my intentions. "Don't do it, Domitius", he said.

I turned to face him. "No matter what happens, do not intervene, tribune", I said while looking him straight in the eye.

The Primus Pilus sighed and issued a curt nod. "I understand and I will obey, Lord Emperor."

I swung down from the saddle, stepped into the water, and started for the opposite bank. "Let Teiwaz be the judge of who the coward is", I said loud enough for the warriors to hear. "Let us settle our grievances the old way", I added, and slid my blade from the scabbard.

Ulfilas knew my reputation. He drew his blade, but rather than to dismount, he spurred his horse into the ford.

Usually, one is at a disadvantage when facing a mounted man on foot, but I had been raised by the horse lords of the Sea of Grass. Ulfilas's gaze darted this way and that as he weighed up whether to ride me down or cut me in half with his heavy blade as he passed. The movement of his hands, knees and eyes betrayed that he had chosen the former.

At the last possible moment, I jumped from the stallion's path - the hooves of the massive horse missing me by mere inches. I shifted my balance, pivoted on my right heel, and my blade flashed at shoulder level. The tip of my sword cleaved the war chief's iron greave and cut deep into his shin.

With a shriek of pain, Ulfilas tumbled from the saddle, the knee-deep water providing some respite from the heavy fall that would have left him winded at best. Having lost his sword in the fall, he feverishly tried to find his blade as I slowly waded towards him.

I noticed a slight grin of triumph, and I was sure that underneath the surface his fist had found the hilt of his sword. "Have mercy", he said, the trace of an evil smile touching the corners of his mouth. "I have no weapon."

My blade flashed, the thrust severing his spine and rendering him unfit to hear my reply, which I gave in any event. "Only a fool would ask for mercy from Eochar the Merciless", I said, wiped my sword on his wet tunic, and slipped it back into the scabbard.

I allowed the current to claim the corpse, and walked to the far side where Goth nobles were watching the spectacle. "Who commands?" I asked.

Two men stepped forward. A tall, grizzled chieftain and a short, powerful warrior with grey streaks in his pleated blonde beard that sported knucklebones of vanquished enemies. Their clothes and armour were of quality and the gold and silver on their muscled arms hinted at their skills with a blade.

"I am Respa, high lord of the Bastarnae", he said, "and this is King Veducus of the Peucini. We speak for the clans of the Goths who have been led astray by the spawn of Tharuarus."

I inclined my head to the nobles. "I have heard your names whispered around campfires. Your reputations precede you."

Veducus issued a sigh. "We are tired of war and death, Lord Eochar", he said. "We wish to speak of peace."

I nodded my agreement. "Come", I said. "Join me on the southern bank and we will do as you suggest."

Chapter 35 – Peace and War (July 270 AD)

"Are you sure?" I asked Thiaper.

"The Carpiani will settle in the land beyond the forested slopes, the place the Romans call Transsilvania. Give the forests south of the mountains to the Peucini and the Bastarnae. They will be a buffer between us and the tribes loyal to the Crow."

"What say you?" I asked the two chieftains.

"The Peucini and the Bastarnae know the way of the woods", Respa replied, and took a swig from his cup. "But we need a place to trade our furs and timber for Roman iron and wheat."

"You will be allowed to operate a marketplace on the southern bank of the Danube", I confirmed.

"What do you wish for in return?" Veducus asked.

"I wish for five thousand of your best mounted warriors to serve in the armies of Rome", I said. "The eldest sons of your nobles will command them on my behalf."

"If the Crow attacks, we will sorely miss their spears", Respa said.

"If Cannabaudes comes, send a rider south", I said. "The legions of Rome will march to support their allies."

***

Later that same evening, Hostilius, Gordas, Cai, Vibius and I shared a meal inside my pavilion.

"Have the savages agreed to your terms?" Hostilius asked while he filled his own cup from an amphora.

"They have till sunrise tomorrow", I said.

I had hardly finished speaking when Diocles appeared in the doorway. "Lord Emperor", he said. "Five thousand Goth *foederati* have arrived at the Illyrian camp. Their commander, Atmon, the son of Respa, wishes to speak with you."

"Send him in", I said.

Moments later, a strapping young warrior pushed aside the door hanging. Four imperial guards escorted him to where we were seated on couches, surrounded by glowing braziers. The young man went down on one knee and inclined his head in respect. "Lord Emperor", he said in the tongue of the Goths. "I bear a gift from my father."

"You are welcome at my hearth, Atmon, son of Respa", I said, and waved him to his feet.

He stood and untied the knots of the bag that was attached to his arming belt. In fear of it being filled with vipers or something of the sort, the praetorians made to stop him.

"Leave him be", I commanded, and the guards retreated a step.

Atmon shook four severed heads onto the wool carpet, which, thankfully, was dyed crimson.

"Who were they?" I asked, raising an eyebrow.

"The chieftains who wished for war instead of peace", he said.

"Thank your father for the generous gift", I replied, and dismissed him with a wave of a hand.

* * *

Three weeks later, Hostilius, Gordas and I stood on a hill to the north and east of Naissus. The elevation afforded us a view of a dirt track meandering along the bottom of a valley in the vast Haemus Mountains. We watched as the last of the Goth wagons disappeared around a far bend of the road. They were heading north to Ratiaria on the Danube. Behind them followed three hundred Illyrians to ensure that none of the barbarians would leave the column and get up to mischief. A similar Illyrian contingent formed the vanguard of the column that stretched for miles and miles along the road.

"I hope that's the last we see of them", Hostilius said.

"When wolves leave their hunting grounds to feast on the flesh of sheep, it is not enough to riddle the culprits with arrows", Gordas mused. "One must seek out the den of the vermin and wring the necks of the cubs because they, too, have lapped up the sweet blood of the herd."

I gave the Hun a sidelong glance.

"You are too merciful, Eochar", he said. "If it were Octar, the valley would be filled with the bleached bones of a nation."

"Would you have had me kill them all?" I asked.

The Hun issued a shrug. "The children of the Goths will remember the fear that they felt in the pits of their stomachs as the battle raged. They will never forget the sea of dead that littered the field of blood. It will remain with them for their entire lives. But the children of their children will discard the warnings of the elders as the ramblings of senile old men. All they will know of Rome is the pierced coins passed from father to son. They will rub the gold between their dirty fingers and greed will drive them to cross the Mother River. Yes, they will come again, but not while we walk this earth."

Hostilius issued a grunt to indicate that he agreed with my barbarian friend.

* * *

"You have done well, husband", Segelinde said when we were alone in our room in the villa. "The Goths and the Carpiani will honour the treaty because they know that if they break their oath, you will cross the river and it will not go well with them. The Romans who choose to remain in Dacia will be treasured for their skills and their trade contacts. They will grow wealthy as a result. The citizens who fear the barbarian yoke will be resettled south of the river on the lands devastated by years of war. They will receive more than they have lost, and they, too, will prosper."

"You are probably the only one who agrees with me", I said. "Hostilius and Gordas wanted me to wipe them out", I added. "Diocles and Vibius's comments suggest that my actions have opened up a rift between me and the senate."

"What does Cai think?" my wife asked.

"Truth is, I don't know", I replied. "As always, he speaks in riddles."

"You should go to Rome, Lucius", she said.

I must have frowned.

"Most Roman emperors ruled from the safety of the Palatine Hill because they feared war", she said. "With you it is the other way round. You dread politics. And you fear what you might do if you discover who ordered the death of Marcus."

"Is it that obvious?" I asked.

She sat down beside me and wrapped an arm around my shoulders. "Rest at home for a few weeks, then we will go to Rome. You have already achieved more than most emperors do in ten years."

"I have achieved nothing apart from surrendering a Roman province to barbarians", I replied. "Marcus, in his short reign, conquered both the Goths and the Alemanni."

Segelinde issued a snicker. "Do you really think that is what your men believe - what the people think? Everyone knows that you were the sword of Claudius Gothicus. It was you who subjugated the Goths and defeated the Alemanni."

"So let us trust that I will be strong enough to withstand the onslaught of the senate", I said, indicating that I would follow her sage advice.

"Just do as you would in war", she said with a twinkle in her eye. "If the conscript fathers do not bend to your will, let them taste your iron."

We shared a smile, not knowing that the spinners of fate were listening to her words. Unlike me, the sisters realised not that Segelinde had jested.

* * *

To be continued.

Historical Note – Main characters

Main characters of the series

Eochar - Lucius Domitius Aurelianus, or Aurelian, as he is better known, I believe, was the most accomplished Roman to ever walk this earth. Some would disagree, which is their right.

In time, all will be revealed, but for now I will leave you with a few quotes from the surviving records.

From the English Translation of the (much-disputed) *Historia Augusta Volume III*:

"Aurelian, born of humble parents and from his earliest years very quick of mind and famous for his strength, never let a day go by, even though a feast-day or a day of leisure, on which he did not practise with the spear, the bow and arrow, and other exercises in arms."

"... he was a comely man, good to look upon because of his manly grace, rather tall in stature, and very strong in his muscles; he was a little too fond of wine and food, but he indulged his passions rarely; he exercised the greatest severity and a discipline that had no equal, being extremely ready to draw his sword."

"..."Aurelian Sword-in-hand," and so he would be identified."

"... in the war against the Sarmatians, Aurelian with his own hand slew forty-eight men in a single day and that in the course of several days he slew over nine hundred and fifty, so that the boys even composed in his honour the following jingles and dance-ditties, to which they would dance on holidays in soldier fashion:

"Thousand, thousand, thousand we've beheaded now.

One alone, a thousand we've beheaded now.

He shall drink a thousand who a thousand slew.

So much wine is owned by no one as the blood which he has shed."

Marcus - Marcus Aurelius Claudius was an actual person, famous in history, and I believe a close friend of Lucius Domitius.

Cai is a figment of my imagination. The Roman Empire had contact with China, or Serica, as it was called then. His origins, training methods and fighting style I have researched in detail. Cai, to me, represents the seldom written about influence of China on the Roman Empire.

Primus Pilus Hostilius Proculus is a fictional character. He represents the core of the legions. The hardened plebeian officer.

Gordas – The fictional Hun/Urugundi general. Otto J Maenschen-Helfen writes in his book, The World of the Huns, that he believes the Urugundi to be a Hunnic tribe. Zosimus, the ancient Byzantine writer, mentions the Urugundi in an alliance with the Goths and the Scythians during the mid-third century AD. (Maenschen-Helfen's book is fascinating. He could read Russian, Persian, Greek and Chinese, enabling him to interpret the original primary texts.)

Vibius Marcellinus was an actual person who later governed a province in the name of Aurelian.

Segelinde – the Gothic princess, is an invention. However, Ulpia Severina, the woman who was married to Aurelian, is not.

Lucius's Contubernia – Ursa, Silentus, Pumilio and Felix. They were not actual people, but represent the common soldiers within the Roman Legions.

Diocles was an actual man. The son of a freedman who became one of the great men in history.

King Bradakos of the Roxolani never lived.

Characters that make a guest appearance.

Postumus was a Roman legate of Batavian descent who emerged as the dominant figure on the Rhine during Valerian's reign.

Haldagates was a Germanic chieftain (mentioned in the Historia Augusta) fighting under the command of Aurelian sometime between 253 AD and 260 AD. He might have been a Frank. His champions, **Hlodwig** and **Fardinanth**, are fictional.

Braduhenna (sometimes Baduhenna) was the name of a Germanic goddess and there is no evidence that she led the Alemanni. Translated, the name means *battle matron*.

Quintillus was the brother of Claudius Gothicus.

Historical Note – Imperator storyline

State of the Roman Empire at the time of this book (July 269 AD to October 270 AD)

The Romans were still licking their wounds after Naissus when news arrived that the Alemanni had invaded Raetia and were on their way to Italy via the Brenner pass. Claudius and Aurelian hurried to Italy where they defeated the Germani at the Battle of Lake Benacus.

The victorious leaders returned to the Balkans soon after to counter an invasion by the Vandals. While gathering their army in Sirmium, Claudius succumbs to the plague.

Could Claudius have been murdered? There is no evidence of this, but knowing the state of the Empire during the third century, I would not be surprised.

The Roman senate elevated Quintillus, Claudius Gothicus's brother, to emperor. He only wore the purple for seventeen days. Aurelian met him in the field, where he was killed by his own men. Some sources state that he opened his own veins.

While Aurelian was dealing with Quintillus, the Goths who had retreated to Mount Haemus managed to break the Roman siege lines. The new emperor met them in the field and crushed them. Soon after, a peace treaty was negotiated between the Romans and the Goths, on Aurelian's terms.

Some sources state that Aurelian abandoned Roman Dacia to the Goths as part of the negotiations. Others believe that he surrendered the province to the Carpiani. When, how and why this happened is the subject of much speculation.

Soon after, the Vandals invaded Pannonia and Aurelian soundly defeated them.

With the Danubian border secured, Aurelian departed for Rome.

Historical Note – Random items

- The Romans used a reaping machine called a *vallus* which required a single draught animal. It cut the ears from the wheat but left the straw on the land. The harvester was invented in Gaul during the first century AD.
- Excessive sweating and sunken eyes are symptoms of dehydration in mules and horses.
- In the time of Aurelian, the main description used by Roman writers for the Germanic peoples is *'Germani'*. In some instances, *'Alemanni'* is used. Who exactly were the Alemanni? I believe that Rome used the description as a collective term for barbarian tribes invading from a certain area. Internally the tribesmen still thought of themselves as affiliated with a specific tribe or a certain war leader.
- In Roman times, long before a system of dykes and drainage systems had been constructed, the Po Valley was an almost impassable swamp. The Athesis and Po could only be crossed at a handful of places, one being Verona. The city was situated where the Via Claudia Augusta (road through the Alps) intersected with the

Via Postumia, an important road connecting the East with the West.

- Around 265 AD, Emperor Gallienus, fearing a barbarian invasion from across the Alps, restored and strengthened the walls of Verona.
- Early Christians under Roman rule greeted each other with the phrase 'maranatha', which means 'the Lord is coming'. After the persecution of Decius and Valerian, Christians under Roman rule enjoyed a period of relative peace which is commonly referred to as *The Little Peace of the Church*.
- In ancient times, white animals were typically sacrificed to celestial gods while black animals were offered to the dark gods of the underworld.
- Germanic dragons are referred to as both *wyrm* and *draca* in ancient writings. One type of dragon is a fire dragon. I made up my own story about its origin.
- According to a local legend, San Colombano, the priest whom the Hermitage of Eremo di San Colombano is named after, slew a dragon. Although Colombano lived in the sixth century it is believed that the story originates from an earlier legend.
- The Black Stone was an ancient shrine in the Roman Forum dating back to the origin of the city.

- Karachun is the Slavic god of death and chaos, commander of the frost. He is often seen in the company of a bear and wolves that do his bidding. Interestingly, his female counterpart is Marzanna. This horse-riding dark crone appears throughout Indo-European mythology, albeit by slightly different names, one of them being Mare. You guessed it - she is the mare in nightmare, the bringer of bad dreams.
- Reading about Karachun, I stumbled upon the origins of Santa Claus, aka 'Sinterklaas'. Most say that he is based upon a good-hearted Christian saint of old. But according to some Eastern European sources, Santa is modelled upon a combination of Karachun and Saint Nicholas of Myra, an archbishop who lived in modern-day Turkey during the third century AD. As part of his duties, he would travel his territories in late winter to collect taxes. If the peasants were unable to pay, he would take their children as slaves to settle their debts - an apparently common practice during that time. It seems that Santa is not the only one with a dark side. Happy snowmen used to be idols that pagan worshippers dedicated to Karachun, the terrible god of death.

- The Marsi, an ancient tribe of central Italy, were also known as the *travelling people*. They, along with the *rootcutters*, were the drug dealers of ancient Rome. Snake-charming was one of their many talents. They worshipped Angitia, the goddess of snakes and healing.
- Deadly webcap mushrooms contain orellanine, a poison that shuts down the kidneys. In some cases, the onset can be slow and the initial symptoms are often flu-like. Apart from dialysis and kidney transplants, there is no cure.
- A deceased emperor's funeral pyre was often lit by his successor.
- In days of old, at the Roman bridge that spanned the Aesontius, there was an altar dedicated to the god of the river. In 1922, a stone inscription was discovered stating that Barbius Montanus, a head centurion of a legion, sacrificed to Aesontius sometime during the third century AD.
- Historians differ about the timing of the abandonment of Roman Dacia. Aurelian was a conqueror at heart, and would not have taken the decision lightly. It might have been that the defences of Dacia were just too far gone and the finances of the Empire stretched too thin.

I believe that Aurelian sacrificed Dacia so that the Empire could be united.

- The first evidence of a Roman army building a marching camp was from the campaigns of Manius Curius Dentatus against Pyrrhus of Epirus in Southern Italy in the year 275 BC. I do not know when the layout was standardised.
- In ancient Rome, when playing dice with the customary four pieces, a throw consisting of four different numbers were apparently called 'Venus', while a losing throw of four number ones were called 'throwing dogs'.
- It is said that *farinata* originated when Roman legionaries roasted chickpea flour on a shield. It must have been a metal shield as the standard issue scutum was made of laminated wood.
- The details of Aurelian's battle against the Goths in the Haemus Mountains are lost. As inspiration for the fictional battle, I used Hannibal's victory over the Vaccaei tribe at the Battle of the Targus around 220 BC.

Historical Note – Place names

Cadianum – Caldiero, Northen Italy.

Athesis River – Adige River.

Pons Drusi – Bolzano, Northern Italy.

Tridentum – Trento, Northern Italy.

Vicetia – Vicenza, Northern Italy.

Patavium – Padua, Northern Italy.

Little Medoacus River – Bacchiglione River.

Secundus's town – Arsiero, Northern Italy.

Dis Pater's Pass (fictional name) – Passo della Borcola, Northern Italy.

The place where Lucius spoke with the Christian monk – Eremo di San Colombano, a hermitage in Trambileno, Italy.

Siscia – Sisak, Croatia.

Savus River – Sava River, Croatia.

Bassiana – Ancient Roman town halfway between Singidunum and Sirmium.

Aesontius River – Isonzo River, Northeastern Ital

Author's Note

I trust that you have enjoyed the fourteenth book in the series.

In many instances, written history relating to this period has either been lost in the fog of time, or it might never have been recorded. That is especially applicable to most of the tribes which Rome referred to as barbarians. These peoples did not record history by writing it down. They only appear in the written histories of the Greeks, Romans, Persians and Chinese, who often regarded them as enemies.

In any event, my aim is to be as historically accurate as possible, but I am sure that I inadvertently miss the target from time to time, in which case I apologise to the purists among my readers.

Kindly take the time to provide a rating and/or a review.

I will keep you updated via my blog with regards to the progress on the fifteenth book in the series.

Feel free to contact me any time via my website. I will respond.

www.HectorMillerBooks.com

Printed in Great Britain
by Amazon